Alison Roberts is a New Zealander, currently lucky enough to be living in the south of France. She is also lucky enough to write for the Mills & Boon Medical Romance line. A primary school teacher in a former life, she is now a qualified paramedic. She loves to travel and dance, drink champagne, and spend time with her daughter and her friends.

TWIN SURPRISE FOR THE ITALIAN DOC

ALISON ROBERTS

MILLS & BOON

First published in Great Britain 2018
by Mills & Boon, an imprint of HarperCollins*Publishers*
1 London Bridge Street, London, SE1 9GF

Large Print edition 2018

© 2018 Alison Roberts

ISBN: 978-0-263-07290-7

MIX
Paper from
responsible sources
FSC® C007454

This book is produced from independently certified
FSC™ paper to ensure responsible forest management. For
more information visit www.harpercollins.co.uk/green.

Printed and bound in Great Britain
by CPI Group (UK) Ltd, Croydon, CR0 4YY

For Sarah, Luke and Brendan,
with lots of love and very fond memories
of our adventures in the Czech Republic. xx

PROLOGUE

'I THINK WE'RE LOST.'

Georgia Bennett had been enjoying the view of this pretty forest road as they wound their way through the Alps that bordered this part of the Czech Republic. It was her companion Kate's turn to drive and it was obvious she was a little out of her comfort zone, which was hardly surprising. Georgia was the crazy one in this friendship—the one that took risks and chased adventures.

And she had every intention of making this one of her most significant adventures ever.

'Whose bright idea was it to enter this international medical rescue competition?' Kate continued. 'Oh, yeah…*yours*…'

'It's an adventure.' Georgia threw a reassuring smile in Kate's direction but reached for the folder that had the maps so she could double check what the satellite navigation device was telling them. 'Admit it—you're loving it already.'

Kate still didn't sound happy. 'Road trips always sound more fun than they actually are. It's a hell of a long way from Scotland to the back of beyond in the Czech Republic. I've never even heard of the town we're trying to find.'

'Rakovi. It's a ski resort. And this is the biggest competition of its kind in the world. I've been hearing about it for years—ever since I became a paramedic.'

Georgia had tried to get a whole team together from her colleagues and persuade the manager of her rescue base to let them take an ambulance on an epic road trip but, despite her best efforts, it hadn't panned out. Then she'd heard about the doctor/paramedic combinations that were allowed and that you could compete using a car. All she'd had to do was persuade Kate. Presenting the whole package as a birthday gift—along with a bottle of really good champagne—had done the trick.

'Well, I've never heard of it.'

'That's because you're a doctor and your lot aren't as adventurous.'

'Hmm…' It sounded like Kate had changed her mind. 'Have we even got out of Poland yet?'

'Ages ago.' Georgia made her tone as soothing as possible. 'It's not far now.'

'We don't want to be late for registration.'

'Don't stress. They've got a couple of hundred teams from about twenty different countries to process. If we're a bit late it'll just mean we don't have to queue for so long.'

Kate slowed again to cross a narrow bridge over a tumbling mountain stream. 'I can't believe we're competing in such a huge field.'

'It's broken up into categories, remember. There'll be paramedic teams with their ambulances from all over Europe. I can't wait till the end where everybody drives in convoy around all the local villages with their lights and sirens on. I've heard it's a memorable experience.' Georgia had come prepared. She had bags of sweets and Scottish-themed toys to throw from the windows for the children that would be lining the edges of the road. It would be such fun to see their faces light up…

Oh, boy…she had small humans on her mind far too much at the moment. She needed to focus.

'Then there are the doctors and medical student teams and other combinations,' she added quickly. 'I just hope there's enough like us to give us our own category, otherwise we'll be competing against teams that have up to four members.'

'I just hope I don't make an idiot of myself. I'm a paediatrician, Georgie. I work in a nice, safe hospital with any amount of resources and backup. You would have been better to pick an emergency specialist.'

'You do plenty of emergency work. And you've lived with me long enough to qualify as an honorary paramedic. You've even been out on the road with me a few times. You'll be brilliant and who cares if we don't win? We're here to have fun, remember? To have an adventure and meet lots of new people and…' Georgia's grin was decidedly mischievous now. 'We're both single and gorgeous. Have you thought about how many men there are going to be at this thing?'

Men who were presumably reasonably intelligent because they were doctors or medical students or paramedics. Successful enough to want to be competitive. Adventurous enough to take on this kind of challenge.

Just the kind of man she would choose to be the father of her child.

Best of all, they would be strangers. From foreign countries. They would never have to know and they would never interfere with her life in the future.

'*Georgie...*' Kate sounded shocked. 'You never give up, do you? You've only just got over the last disaster and you're ready to do it again?'

The reminder of how gutting the last relationship mess had been was the last thing Georgia wanted to think about. Or maybe it was a good thing because she could feel her resolve strengthening. She was thirty-six now—a year older than Kate—and she didn't have the time or inclination to jump through any more messy relationship hoops.

She wanted a baby.

Not that she was about to confess her master plan, even to her very best friend who'd been her housemate for years. Kate was too proper. She had set ideas about the way things should be in life and wasn't likely to approve of Georgia's intentions. A one-off, throw-away comment she had made a while back about a man only being essential for as long as it might take to conceive had been enough to tell her that. Kate had been appalled.

So she made her tone as offhand as she could. 'Oh, I have no intention of falling for someone.' And wasn't that the truth?

Inspiration struck. 'What's that saying? The best way to get over a man is to get under another one?'

At least she'd made Kate laugh. That wouldn't be the case if she'd guessed the truth.

'Casual sex has never appealed to me.'

'Yeah…you're so old school, Kate. An ultimate romantic.' This was good. She could divert the attention to Kate's love life—or lack of it—instead of her own. 'You really believe that you're going to see 'the one' across a crowded room and it'll be love at first sight and a happy-ever-after with a few bluebirds fluttering over the carpet of rose petals and—'

'Oh, stop it...,' Kate growled. But she didn't sound cross. Her tone was more concerned than anything. 'Just be careful, hon. Okay?'

'Of course.' Georgia breathed a sigh of relief but that seemed to earn a sharp glance from Kate.

'You have given up on that hare-brained scheme you came up with after that bastard, Rick, walked out, haven't you?'

Uh-oh... 'I have no idea what you're talking about.'

'Oh, yes, you do. The one where you gave up on men completely and were going to have a baby all by yourself?'

Georgia pretended to be distracted by the map in her hands. She couldn't afford to allow Kate to get suspicious. She had the lid firmly in place over her own doubts about what she was planning and it would be too easy to get talked out of it if that lid got lifted.

She could almost feel that biological clock ticking more loudly than ever. Or was it her heart thumping? Excitement…or trepidation?

She cleared her throat. 'Well, obviously I haven't given up on men *completely*. And I'm over Rick. He's ancient history—like all the others.' Oh, man…she had to change the subject of conversation. Nerves were kicking in and the feeling was not pleasant.

She told herself to calm down. It was just an option—she didn't have to follow through with her plan if she wasn't sure. Maybe she wouldn't meet anyone suitable. And, even if she did, what were the odds of getting pregnant with a single encounter anyway? She wasn't even sure that it was the best time of the month, given that her cycle wasn't that regular.

There were other reasons to be here. Exciting reasons. And there was no need to continue with any hazardous chatting either. Georgia had seen the perfect distraction.

'Ooh, look…a signpost. We're only fifteen kilometres away.'

'Halleluiah. The end is in sight.'

'Nah…the *beginning* is in sight.' Georgia stretched her arms above her head and gave a whoop. 'Bring it on.'

CHAPTER ONE

YES...

This was all shaping up to be even better than Georgia could have imagined.

While she was well aware that she was a part of the growing percentage of women succeeding in demanding careers like paramedicine, there were hundreds and hundreds of people here and it seemed like the majority of them were men.

The kind of men that had always stood out from the crowd for her. Intelligent, confident men who were caring enough to devote their working lives to caring for others. Born leaders who could wear a uniform like a second skin rather than an advertisement of achievement or authority.

One of them could be exactly the kind of man she would choose to be the father of her child.

The sense of unease that touched the back of

her neck and rippled down her spine was becoming familiar but Georgia had come up with a
way to shrug it off with what seemed a perfectly
feasible argument in her defence. She wasn't the
only woman who was prepared to embrace the
decision to bring a child into the world without
a partner.

She could have taken what was becoming an
accepted route to parenthood by paying for the
services of a sperm bank and the initial part of
that process would be to peruse the profiles of
available candidates. She would be making judge-
ments based on physical attributes like height and
colouring. Academic qualifications and profes-
sion could indicate levels of intelligence and determination and interests in things like sport or
music could offer an insight into attitudes or tal-
ents.

She could well end up doing exactly that but
what put her off that route to parenthood was the
fact that it would be recorded. Traceable. The risk
of that knowledge being used to interfere with
her life was probably small enough to be insig-

nificant but Georgia knew only too well how damaging that interference was capable of being. Why take the risk if it was possible to eliminate it completely?

She had convinced herself that all she was planning to do was to peruse profiles in a much less clinical fashion, by means of personal interaction.

The thornier issue of consent was more difficult to shrug off, of course, but there wasn't any point in facing that one unless she found a suitable candidate. Given her list of requirements, it was quite possible that even this best-case scenario of potentially great men wouldn't provide exactly what she was looking for.

What with getting through the registration protocol and transferring their luggage to their accommodation, the time since she and Kate had arrived at the rally had been a bit too busy to get more than a very general impression of their fellow competitors but that had just changed. Standing in a crowded dining hall, holding her dinner tray, Georgia found herself joining Kate's attempt to locate two empty spaces at a table. Except that it was the array of faces capturing her attention instead of any empty chairs. Surprisingly, many of those faces were looking back at them and they didn't seem to be simply curious glances that might be assessing competitors. There were smiles to be seen, along with raised eyebrows that suggested friendliness, if not interest.

Like that very tall guy, with a mop of sun-streaked blond curls and a cheeky grin. The tilt of his head was an unmistakeable invitation to claim the extra space at *his* table.

Georgia smiled back.

'There's some space on that table,' she told Kate, leading the way. She smiled again as they got closer. 'Do you mind if we join you guys?'

'Please do.' He looked delighted. 'I'm Dave. This is Ken and that's Sally, who's stuffing her face there.'

'You're from Australia, right?'

'No. New Zealand.' Dave sighed heavily. 'Everybody thinks our accent is the same but it really isn't.' He grinned at Georgia. 'No mistaking yours. You're Scottish.'

'I am.' Georgia took the empty seat right beside Dave.

New Zealand… It was a country that conjured up images of clean, green forests and pristine beaches—like advertisements for healthy lifestyles. Even better, it was a country on the opposite side of the globe. About as far from Scotland as possible. It was impossible not to register that that fact ticked one of the first boxes on the list of requirements she had drawn up on her potential master plan.

The plan that had suddenly become rather more than just a half-baked idea, in fact.

The dumplings on her plate were rather dense and speckled with something green that could be parsley. Dave appeared to be enjoying his meal and Georgia was never fussy with her food so she took a large bite and found that the dumplings were actually better than they looked, especially with a covering of the gravy they were swimming in.

She glanced sideways as she loaded her fork again. 'I like your uniforms. Are you paramedics?'

'Yeah…you guys?'

'I'm a paramedic. Kate's a doctor. Is this your first time here?'

'Sure is. Never seen anything like it.'

'Where are you based at home? City or country?'

'Auckland. Biggest city in the country. And up there in the top cities of the world to live in. You should come and visit sometime.'

'Oh? What's so great about Auckland?'

The attractions seemed to focus on fabulous beaches, a great night life and the best food and coffee the world had to offer. Sally and Ken were keen to tell her about what a great place it was to work in the ambulance service as well, but Auckland wasn't a likely destination to add to any future travel plans, as far as Georgia was concerned.

Especially if any more boxes on that mental list were going to get ticked and that was apparently happening without her even consciously thinking about it. Dave was tall, which made a good genetic balance for her own slightly below average stature. He was definitely good looking and there was a gleam in those blue eyes that suggested intelligence. As a bonus, his camaraderie with his teammates told her that he wasn't any kind of sociopath.

Dave seemed, on first impression, to be a very nice guy and Georgia experienced another pang of guilt that she could even be thinking along these lines. Was she really planning to cultivate a friendship enough to use someone for such a selfish purpose? Getting pregnant accidentally was common enough to be almost normal but it was more than a little disturbingly immoral to *plan* such an event.

She glanced at Kate, almost hoping that enough telepathy existed between them that her friend would sense the secret list-ticking and deliver a hint of shock with some raised eyebrows and then a frown, or perhaps a headshake, of total disapproval.

But Kate wasn't even looking in her direction. She seemed to be focussed on her meal and wasn't joining in with the conversation around her. Maybe she was more out of her comfort zone than Georgia had anticipated when she'd persuaded her to come to this competition. Kate was incredibly clever and hardworking and the best friend Georgia had ever had, but nobody could say she was overly adventurous. Or even spontaneous. If there was going to be a break in her normal routines, Kate liked to be able to plan how to cope with it. Making a plan that would turn her whole life upside down would be so unthinkable that Georgia had known instantly that it had been a mistake to even voice her idea of bypassing the search for a suitable partner and moving straight on to parenthood.

Or maybe Kate was thinking about the old friend from medical school she thought she'd spotted in the crowd at registration. The news that he was now married had been disappointing. Thanks to the latest disaster of being unceremoniously dumped by Rick, Georgia was completely over the idea of finding the love of her life but her flatmate was still a believer and, if anybody deserved the happy-ever-after of the full package, it was Kate.

Perhaps the vibe of wishing the best for her had transmitted itself to Kate because she finally looked up from her meal. She glanced from Georgia to Dave and back again, a subtle quirk of her eyebrow confirming what Georgia already knew—that Dave was interested and it would be very easy to turn this chance meeting into something more—but even that didn't provoke any hint of disapproval.

Kate started chatting to Sally and Ken then, clearly interested in hearing about what it was like to live and work in New Zealand. Seeing that she seemed more relaxed about being here allowed Georgia to release a small sigh of relief. Maybe Kate was making an effort to embrace this adventure and the next couple of days would be a lot of fun for both of them.

And maybe that was exactly what Georgia needed to do. To focus on this competition for what it was—an opportunity to demonstrate her skills to the best of her ability. Kate was smart enough to be right most of the time and the plan that had seemed like an epiphany a few weeks ago, however half-baked it had been, *was* a hare-brained scheme.

And wrong?

With a small, inward sigh, she joined in the conversation and avoided looking at Dave again until she had finished her meal. By the time they all filed out of the dining room on the way to the pre-competition briefing she had decided that Dave, despite how cute he might be, was safe. After only one candidate, she was done with her personal profile testing.

She didn't need Kate's disapproval because she had just tapped into plenty of her own.

Men who contributed to sperm banks were doing so with the full knowledge that they could be fathering children they would never know. Making an assumption that what someone didn't know couldn't hurt them was irresponsible and… and unacceptable.

All the men here were safe.

She was done with any list-ticking. The master plan had been scrapped.

'Between eleven-thirty and midnight tonight, you will all receive your list of events.'

Georgia felt her heart pick up its rate as a squiggle of excitement tickled her gut. This was really happening. She'd heard about this competition years ago, when she'd been training to become a paramedic, and it had always been a dream. *This* was why she was here and the crazy idea of hooking up with someone and possibly going home pregnant was no longer even remotely interesting.

'You will be given the GPS coordinates of the scenario and a start time,' the official continued. 'Please be there at least ten minutes before that time. If you are late, you will not be admitted and you will not be marked in that section of the competition.'

Georgia elbowed Kate, who was standing close beside her in this very crowded room. 'No chance of that happening,' she whispered. 'Not when I'm with you.'

The comment should have earned the kind of eye-roll that Kate bestowed automatically whenever she was reminded of her compulsion to obey rules but, instead, she received a quick grin. Maybe Kate was feeling as excited as she was now that this was actually beginning. Or would be in a few hours.

Starting at six a.m. tomorrow, there would be twelve tasks for each team to complete within twenty-four hours, with time allowed for rest and meal breaks along the way. A final warning about possible elimination from the competition if any teams were found to be sharing information about the tasks completed the briefing and a babble of conversation broke out amongst a shifting audience.

To Georgia's surprise, Kate immediately turned to the man standing on her other side.

'What section are you in?' she asked. 'All doctors? Doctors and med students?'

Her body language suggested the ease of an

old friendship so Georgia realised that this man had to be the one Kate had told her about. Luke?

'Doctor/paramedic.' He put his arm over the shoulders of his companion. 'This is Matteo Martini. Italian paramedic extraordinaire.'

Georgia's gaze shifted. And then something a lot bigger shifted inside her chest.

This Italian paramedic had to be the most gorgeous man she had ever seen in her entire life. Well over six feet tall, his strong features were softened by a frame of soft waves of black hair and his eyes looked like the darkest, most luxurious chocolate you could imagine. And that smile…just crooked enough to give a hint of playfulness. Mischief even?

Whatever. The net effect was drop-dead sexy.

'Ooh…' The sound was almost an approving hum and Georgia felt as if her body was shifting itself a bit closer, even though she knew she hadn't moved. And then her mouth opened without giving her time to think about whatever words she wanted to produce. What did emerge was vaguely appalling.

'A martini? Yes, please… Extra-dry—with an olive.'

She saw the flash of surprise in those chocolate-coloured eyes but then it vanished in the wave of laughter that Georgia managed to join in with, making her ridiculously flirtatious comment no more than a joke.

'This is Georgie,' Kate said. 'My paramedic partner.'

It seemed the most natural thing in the world to fall into step beside Matteo as Kate and Luke led the way to the bar where everyone was going to wait for the scenario list and start times to be handed out.

She felt small beside this solid male figure. And a bit embarrassed, to be honest, after her overly enthusiastic response to their introduction.

Matteo seemed perfectly at ease. He bent his head so that his voice was like a soft, teasing growl intended only for her ears.

'So…you and me, then?'

Oh, *help*… If her response to their introduction had been flirtatious, this was more like blatant seduction and the reaction of her body to both the sound of his voice and the implied invitation was like nothing Georgia had ever experienced. She'd met this man less than a minute ago and already the attraction was so powerful she wanted…

An upward glance gave her direct contact with those extraordinary eyes.

Oh, man…she wanted *everything*. The sheer force of such an unexpected response to a stranger was actually alarming enough to make her break the eye contact within the space of a heartbeat.

And she didn't trust herself to say a single word.

Even more disturbingly, she could feel a faint fluttering sensation that she recognised only too well.

Hope…

That this was *it*. That perhaps she had found the person she had been searching for. *Her* person.

The mental stamp was forceful enough to squash the flutter.

How many times? It wasn't even that long since her heart had been broken for what she had sworn would be the very last time. She was not going to be stupid enough to take even a single step

down that path. The one that ended with someone waiting inside a pretty church, bathed in all
the promise of happily-ever-after.

No and no and *no*.

'The competition,' Matteo offered helpfully
into the short silence. 'We're in the same category. We both have a doctor for a partner.'

'Oh…that's true.' There was a very different
sensation dampening the flicker of desire now.
Disappointment?

For heaven's sake, Georgia told herself firmly.
Get a grip…

Matteo paused by the entrance to the bar to
allow her to go in first. He smiled at her.

'I intend to win,' he said.

Georgia couldn't help herself. 'So do I,' she
warned.

This time she didn't look away. Neither did
Matteo. He was still smiling.

'Do you always get what you want, Georgie?'

The way his accent changed her name into
something rather more exotic sent a shiver
down her spine. The gleam in his eyes suggested

amusement but there was a warmth there, too, that made her feel like he would be more than happy to help her get what she wanted, even if it meant sacrificing something he wanted himself.

She shook her head sadly.

'Not always.'

But she was smiling as well.

Maybe—this time—she would. The question was simply what she wanted more.

The first prize in this competition?

Or Matteo Martini?

CHAPTER TWO

'WHAT'S THE TIME?'

'Five past eight.'

'We're early.' Matteo Martini sighed. Waiting had never been his forte.

It was an exercise in self-control. A tightrope to balance on between the need to follow rules and gather information and the desire to act. To help someone in trouble. To save a life perhaps…

This wasn't a real life situation, however, which made it impossible to gather any clues about what was to come from a radio conversation or up-dated pager messages. All they had was a mini-mal briefing sheet that had given them the GPS coordinates for the scene and that they would be assessing a thirty-five-year-old woman with ab-dominal pain.

Their tasks were listed as well and they had to

assess the scene, examine and treat the patient, define a working diagnosis and means of transport if necessary, within a time limit of eleven minutes.

This was all about following rules. Waiting in their vehicle until it was their turn to enter what looked like a very ordinary village house to face their first scenario of this emergency response competition.

'Doesn't look like much.' Luke sounded disappointed. 'You sure we're in the right place?'

'*Sì. Assolutamente.*' Matteo pointed through the windscreen. 'That car parked over there is a competitor. It's got the numbers. And a light on the roof, like ours. And the flags are...'

'Scottish,' Luke murmured.

The tension of having to wait had just got a whole lot easier as Matteo felt himself being pulled back into the unexpected delight of meeting Georgia Bennett last night. What a stroke of luck it had been that her partner for this competition was an old friend of Luke's. He didn't even have to make an effort to get an introduction to a woman who would have caught his eye no matter how big a crowd she was in.

There was a glow of energy about Georgia that made him think of adventure. Fun. In combination with that tumble of dark blonde curly hair and those hazel-brown eyes that had rather fascinating flecks of gold, she was irresistible. Given their passion for a shared career, that easy conversation over a drink or two had been a bonus. And by the end of the evening, when they'd split up to study the lists of scenarios that had been handed out to the waiting teams, Matteo had been left with the conviction that the attraction he'd discovered was mutual.

Whether they would have the chance to explore that attraction any further was an enticing possibility but Matteo wasn't going to allow it to distract him for any longer than a delicious minute or two. He had, in fact, dismissed it from his mind completely well before their start time of eight-fifteen a.m.

Until he saw the two women emerge from the house, that was. Until Georgia spotted them waiting in their vehicle and raised her hand to wave at him.

Until she smiled…

'Be nice to have an idea of what we're heading into,' Luke said. 'They weren't giving away any clues, were they?'

'And neither should they,' Matteo said sternly. 'That would be dishonest.'

'Not exactly.' Luke's tone was thoughtful. 'Dishonesty is when you fail to tell the truth. Breaking the rules of the competition to give someone else an advantage would be dishonourable rather than dishonest.'

'Hmm…' Matteo absorbed the correction. 'They are both unacceptable.'

Dishonesty was at the top of his list of despicable human traits. Right up there with cruelty and violence, particularly when children were involved.

'Too right they are,' Luke agreed.

Thrusting his arms through the straps of his pack of gear, Matteo had another moment of distraction.

Had he been a little *too* honest with Georgia during that conversation last night? He'd probably talked about his family with rather too much enthusiasm, hadn't he? If he had wanted to encourage any attraction on her part, he should have stuck to talking about the more exciting exploits of his career as a helicopter paramedic instead of how close he was to his mother and his sisters. Good grief, he'd had to blink tears from his eyes when he'd told her about how much of a thrill it had been to welcome his latest nephew into the world recently.

Weirdly, that slightly cringe-making moment of distraction became an advantage a very short time later, when the two men found themselves in a confusing scenario of a party going on in the house. If the memory of holding that newborn baby hadn't been still there in the back of his mind, would he have been so quick to run up the stairs when they'd heard there was a pregnant girl having stomach pains? And maybe he wouldn't have put quite the same amount of passion into resuscitating a baby who wasn't breathing if he hadn't been imagining that it could have been his sister as the terrified young mother.

In any case, there had been nods of satisfaction from the judges and both he and Luke felt far more confident when they arrived at their second scenario, which clearly had nothing to do with childbirth. Their patient was a middle-aged man who was curled up on a bed and groaning loudly as they entered the room. He was also holding a plastic bucket.

'He's been sick.' The woman who'd met them at the door had explained that she was his wife. 'He got this terrible back pain all of a sudden and then he started vomiting.'

'Could you get some baselines, please, Matt?' Luke was taking the lead on this scenario. 'I'll see what I can find out with the history.' He crouched down beside the bed.

'Show me where this pain is.'

The man put his hand on his side, under his ribs but then moved it towards his abdomen and into his groin.

'Is it the first time you've experienced it?'

'Yes.'

'How bad is it? On a scale of zero to ten, with zero being no pain at all and ten being the worst you can imagine?'

'Ten…' He groaned again. 'And I feel sick…'

'We'll give you something to help with that in just a minute.'

Matteo held a tympanic thermometer close to their patient's ear.

'Temperature's normal,' the nearest judge informed him as he continued taking baseline recordings. 'He's tachycardic at one-twenty, respirations are twenty-four and his blood pressure is one-thirty over ninety.'

Matteo caught Luke's glance. With a normal temperature, infection was less likely to be a cause of this pain so a diagnosis like appendicitis or diverticulitis could be ruled out for the moment. What was needed now was pain relief. He collected everything he needed to insert an IV line and put a tourniquet on the man's arm.

'The IV line is in.' The judge nodded.

'Have you had any trouble urinating?' Luke

asked now. 'Is it painful or have you noticed any-thing different?'

'It hurts,' the man replied. 'And it's very dark.'

Luke glanced at Matteo, who nodded. The di-agnosis and their management now appeared simple.

'We think you might have a kidney stone,' Luke said. 'And it's blocking your ureter and causing this pain. We'll give you something for the pain and then we'll take you to hospital. Are you al-lergic to anything that you know of?'

'No.'

Matteo was already going through the motions of drawing up the morphine.

'What dosage are you administering?' one of the judges asked.

'We'll start with five milligrams,' Luke replied. 'We can top that up if the pain scale isn't reduced to less than five.'

The judge nodded. 'The drug has been admin-istered.'

Matteo began tidying up and Luke was check-ing their briefing sheet that gave a list of available hospitals and means of transport. They needed to choose the most appropriate option, which ranged from leaving the patient where he was, transport by helicopter or ambulance to the nearest general hospital, a higher-level hospital or a specialised centre.

Matteo dropped the packages of IV gear back into his pack and turned to pick up the blood-pressure cuff.

To his horror, he could see that their patient now seemed to be having trouble breathing and he was clutching at his chest.

'Luke…' The word was a warning. He reached out to take the man's pulse. 'Do you have chest pain, sir?'

Their patient didn't respond. His head fell back against the pillow and he was gasping for breath.

Luke was still processing this unexpected twist in their scenario.

'Do we see any skin changes?'

'You see redness appearing,' a judge said. 'And hives.'

Nothing more than a glance between Luke and Matteo was needed.

'Anaphylaxis to morphine,' Matteo agreed quietly. 'I'll get a bag of fluids up. And we need some adrenaline, stat.'

They both worked swiftly to counter a potentially fatal situation, administering drugs, getting their patient on oxygen and a cardiac monitor. Within a couple of minutes the judges were nodding with satisfaction and declared the scenario complete. They just wanted to ask some questions.

'What is your hospital of choice for this patient?'

'Hospital A,' Luke told them. 'They have an internal medicine department and an intensive care unit and they are the closest.'

'And what is the most important information to pass on about your patient?'

'That he has a previously undiscovered allergy to morphine. We will write it on his notes and make sure the information is received by everyone we speak to. We will also advise the patient that it would be a good idea to wear a Medic-Alert bracelet from now on.'

'That was good.' Matteo slapped Luke on the back as they left the house. 'I might not have thought of recommending the bracelet.'

'I was too slow to spot the change in our patient's condition. Well done, you.'

Matteo grinned at his friend. 'We make a good team.'

'We've got a break now, haven't we? About an hour?'

'We should use it to do the driving test.'

'Okay.' Matteo was looking forward to this test. He might work on helicopters now but his early years as a paramedic had been on the road and he loved the challenge of driving fast and doing it well.

A gravelled area beside the river that ran through this village had been cordoned off for this part of the competition and a line of orange road cones marked the course. They could see an ambulance completing the test as they arrived, clouds of dust billowing as it snaked around the cones at high speed and then came to a sudden halt between the cones marking the end of the course.

Another car was waiting for its turn.

The car with the Scottish flags.

And there it was again…

Distraction. A delicious buzz of anticipation at the knowledge he would be seeing Georgia again.

It had always been a given that he would thoroughly enjoy coming to this competition again.

A smile took over his face as he spotted Georgia sitting in the driver's seat of the girls' vehicle. He just hadn't realised how much better it would be this time.

'Cute,' he murmured.

The swift glance from Luke held a note of surprise. Or maybe concern. Did he think that Matteo was here to chase women rather than focus on their performance? He thought fast, putting a casual smile on his face as he shifted his gaze from the woman in the driver's seat. 'I didn't notice that before.'

The look of surprise increased as Luke raised his eyebrows. 'You mean Georgia? Or Kate?'

Okay. Maybe his interpretation of that glance had been accurate.

He hoped his laugh was as casual as his smile.

'Oh, the girls are both cute but that wasn't what I was looking at. Have you seen what is tied to the front of their car?'

It was a stuffed toy bear that was wearing a kilt and holding a set of bagpipes.

Matteo rolled down his window and pointed to the toy, raising his voice so that Georgia could hear him. 'He is going to get dirty, I think.'

'All part of the fun.' Georgia was grinning at him as she called back. Holding his gaze.

Mio Dio… That smile. The sparkle in those eyes. It was enough to make Matteo's breath catch. For an odd warmth to ignite in his gut and then spread all the way through his body.

What was it about this woman that was so different?

So compelling?

Could Georgia feel this same unusual level of

attraction? Possibly not, by how focussed she clearly was on what she was about to do.

'Which one of you is going to do the driving? You're only allowed one person in the vehicle.'

There was a hint of something in her eyes. A challenge perhaps? Or did she want to watch him showing what he was capable of?

His lips twitched in a suppressed smile. He would be more than happy to demonstrate any skill she might be interested in—and he was apparently good at many things that women liked…

But did Luke want to do the driving?

No. His companion was already unclipping his safety belt.

'You do it,' he said to Matteo. 'You've got far more experience with emergency driving skills than I have. I'll wait with Kate.'

'Cool.' Matteo nodded as Luke got out of the car. He could focus now.

He needed to know exactly what was required to make sure he aced this particular test.

He needed to make sure he impressed Georgia…

* * *

'You're a bit quiet, Georgie. Not worried about the next task, are you?'

'Not at all. I was just thinking about that driving test. I could have done better.'

Georgia wished she'd done better. She might not have been able to see his face but she'd *known* that Matteo was watching her and the effect had been to make her very uncharacteristically self-conscious. Clumsy even. She had felt his gaze on her like a physical touch of his hand on her skin and the hyperawareness it had created had messed with her concentration. How embarrassing had it been to send those road cones flying on her first attempt at the serpentine? It wasn't until she had been able to shut him out of her thoughts that she'd been able to demonstrate what she was capable of.

'You did great.' Kate's tone was reassuring.

'Not as great as Matteo,' Georgia muttered.

Kate grinned. 'He was something else, wasn't he? I've never seen anyone drive like that. *So* fast. And he didn't touch a single cone.'

Georgia scowled. 'Thanks for reminding me.'

Kate laughed. 'Let it go. I'll bet there are other things he's not as good at. He's a boy. And he's Italian. Maybe he had a Ferrari when he was a teenager.'

Oh, man, there was an image to play with. A younger version of Matteo Martini. With much longer hair perhaps, behind the wheel of a very fast car. With that easy grin on his face and only one hand on the wheel because his other arm would be over the shoulders of the girl in the passenger seat. Because there *would* be a girl, no doubt about that. Or maybe his hand would be resting on her leg, his thumb making lazy circles on that sensitive skin on her inner thigh. The girl would be smiling, too, of course. Georgia certainly would be...

It was ridiculous to experience a twinge of something so easily recognisable as envy.

No, it was even worse than envy. This felt like jealousy, thanks to the way Georgia's eyes were narrowing. She shook her head to stop it happening.

'What's the next task about?'

'It's called "School Bag". We're being called to a teacher who has tripped over a school bag and is lying on the floor, not moving. She's unconscious but breathing. Head injury, do you think?'

'I'm sure it won't be that simple. We'll have to make sure we rule out other causes of unconsciousness. Was the fall the cause or did she fall because of something else?'

'Like a cardiac event.'

'Yes. Or hypoglycaemia, drug overdose, a stroke, seizures, anaphylaxis, alcohol. It's a long list.'

'Let's hope there's someone around who can tell us exactly what happened. We need to know how she was acting immediately before she fell.'

The only other people in the classroom with the unconscious woman, however, apart from the silent judges, were a group of young children who were taking every advantage of their teacher being unable to control them. Some were having a race around the room, jumping from one desk top to another. One was ripping pages from a textbook. They were all shouting and laughing.

The teacher was lying face down near the blackboard. A school satchel was close to her feet, spilling its contents of an apple, drink bottle and box of pencils. Kate felt for a pulse on their patient's neck the moment they got close enough.

'Hello…can you hear me?'

'You have no response,' a judge informed her. 'The heart rate is one hundred and twenty.'

They rolled their patient carefully so that they could protect her airway. The noise in the class-room increased and Kate was hit on the head by a ball of screwed-up paper. Georgia's head swerved and caught the culprit—the boy who'd been ripping pages from the book. He grinned at Georgia.

An impish grin beneath a wild mop of curly hair. Such a cute kid, she had to stop herself grinning back. Instead, she jumped to her feet and tried to find her sternest expression. If they couldn't get this scene under control, it was going to make it impossible to do their job well.

'Enough,' she shouted. 'All of you kids come here. At *once.*'

A chair toppled with a crash in the sudden silence that followed. One by one, the children came closer. They were all acting so well, with their heads down to show that they knew they were in trouble. One little girl, with huge blue eyes and long plaits, was biting her lip and looking so scared that Georgia just wanted to give her a cuddle.

'It's okay,' she told them. 'But you have to stop being naughty. Your teacher is sick. Did anyone see what happened?'

'She fell over,' one of the children said.

'And before that?'

The children shook their heads. One boy turned away and pushed another one, who pushed back. Georgia caught a third boy who stepped past her, poised to start running again. From the corner of her eye, she could see Kate taking some baseline measurements, including blood glucose. Then she looked at one of the judges.

'Is there someone available who could look after these children?'

'There is a school caretaker outside the room.' A nod from the judge was the signal for the young actors to leave the scene. The boy who'd thrown the paper ball grinned at Georgia again as he left and this time she did return the smile. Along with a quick wink.

'Blood glucose too low to register,' Kate said behind her. 'Skin is cold and clammy and she's still tachycardic.'

'Cool. I'll set up for a glucose infusion.' Georgia turned back to the task as the door closed behind the last of the children. They could work in peace now but there was a part of her that was missing the energy that had been in the room a moment ago.

An energy that only children could provide. That wholehearted enthusiasm for being alive that adults learned to control too well sometimes. Taking advantage of an opportunity for adventure was a hallmark of a happy child and it always seemed to involve either laughter or tears—a pendulum that could swing unpredictably.

Georgia loved the unexpected.

And she loved kids. Even more than babies. She'd had always had dreams of having a whole bunch of them. A messy house and lots of noise with hopefully more laughter than tears. A frantic routine of cooking, cleaning, cuddles and school runs to deliver her little tribe to classrooms just like this one.

She had a job to do now that had nothing to do with small people and the fragment of that dream that the extras in this scenario had prompted was easy enough to push aside.

But it was a reminder that it was still there. Getting stronger with every passing week. If she was going to achieve even a part of that dream she was going to have to do it soon.

And having a kid you could take to school had to start in a very different place.

With having a baby.

And that brought her straight back to the plan she had just abandoned on moral grounds—of using this competition as an opportunity to start that journey to parenthood.

Georgia dismissed that line of thought easily as well as she taped the cannula to their patient's arm as evidence that an IV line had been established.

As they monitored the effects of their treatment, she tried to think of anything they might be missing that could be another twist in this scenario.

'She's not wearing a Medic-Alert bracelet, is she?'

'No.' Kate moved the collar of the shirt their patient was wearing. 'Or a necklace.'

'Can you check her bag? Or the drawer in her desk? It would be useful to know what medication she's on. Is she using insulin or medication to lower her blood sugar? She might have overdosed.'

Kate did find a packet of tablets in the teacher's bag but they weren't what they might have expected.

'These are antidepressants, aren't they?'

'Yes.'

The woman lying on the floor began to move and she groaned softly.

'Your patient's blood glucose level is returning to normal,' one of the judges said. 'What is your plan for transport?'

Georgia thought fast. 'We will transport her to hospital. She has no one here to watch her and we don't know what her normal regime is for her diabetes control.'

'Which hospital do you choose?'

'Hospital B.'

'Why?'

'Because it's a higher-level hospital and there are psychiatric services available. The fact that she's taking antidepressants suggests that there are additional issues for this patient that might be affecting her control of her disease.'

The judges nod was pleased. So was Kate's.

'Good job,' she whispered, as they left the scene. 'I probably would have picked Hospital A because it was the closest. And I might not have thought to check her bag either.'

'You get patients delivered to you with a hand-over of any available information. I guess I'm just used to searching for clues.' Georgia shoved the bulky pack of gear into the back of the car. 'It's one of the things I love about my job—getting to play detective on scene along with being the medic.'

Matteo shared her passion for this job. He was probably as good at playing detective on scene as he was at emergency driving. They'd never run out of fascinating things to talk about, would they?

Oh, boy…this was getting worse. She was actually thinking in terms of for ever? Of growing old together and still not running out of conversation?

'You have to deal with all the distractions, too,' Kate added. 'Those kids were doing my head in to start with.'

The bunch of children was being ushered back into the building now, probably to prepare for the next scenario. As Kate and Georgia drove away, they spotted a car they recognised heading towards the school.

'I think those boys are stalking us.'

Kate's lips twitched as if she was trying not to smile. 'Just coincidence.' But she turned her head to watch the car disappear. 'I wonder how they'll cope with finding a riot going on.'

Georgia lapsed into silence. Matteo would cope very well. He probably wouldn't even need to shout at the children to get their attention and gain control of the scene. He'd only need to smile at them and they would be eating out of his hand because they'd know how much he loved kids.

And he *did* love kids. A large part of the conversation they'd had over drinks last night, when Kate and Luke had been talking quietly, had been about his family. About how much he adored his sister's children and what a thrill the recent birth of a new nephew had been. It sounded as if the entire Martini clan had been at the hospital to welcome that new arrival and Georgia hadn't missed the way Matteo had spoken about his other sisters and his mother. She could have sworn he'd actually had tears in his eyes at one point. Family was clearly of the utmost importance in his life.

And wouldn't he make the best father? He would be totally devoted to his children and there would be a huge, extended family in the wings to make every milestone a glorious celebration.

If that was what Georgia was looking for, Matteo would be perfect.

A few years ago even, when she'd still had the dream that she could find her perfect partner and be totally confident that her own children would never face the kind of fear that had poisoned her own childhood, Matteo would have stood out as being exactly what she was searching for. Gorgeous and confident and super-smart. She'd been more than impressed to learn about his postgraduate qualifications in resuscitation and aeromedical transportation.

But the last remnants of that dream had come crashing down in the wake of the brutal ending of her last relationship. Her heart had been broken for the last time and she knew not to trust that tiny flutter of hope that had come from nowhere when she'd seen this gorgeous Italian for the first time.

His passion for his family was actually a massive negative in the grand scheme of things because if the worst happened, she would be facing an army of opponents if she wanted to protect her children. And she knew that fighting even one could be too many.

It was an automatic gesture to turn her arm a little whenever this memory surfaced. To see the jagged scar that remained from the arm that had been so badly broken when she was only five years old. To feel a shiver of that terror when her birth father had arrived to claim her and the struggle to drag her from her mother's arms had turned vicious.

Not that it had surfaced much in the last few years, because Georgia had believed she would choose a good man and could rewrite history, but her choices had proved untrustworthy. And, okay, maybe Rick had only been verbally vicious when he'd ended their relationship but that had been more than enough to stir the memories. Her 'father' had been just as quick to cause pain with words as anything physical.

And Italians had a reputation for having quick

tempers, didn't they? Imagine having to face an entire family of angry Italians?

Kate's voice broke into her thoughts. 'Penny for them?'

'Huh?'

'You're miles away. What's up?'

'I'm just hungry,' Georgia said. 'It must be time for lunch, isn't it?'

Kate checked their schedule.

'Yep. We've got a break for over an hour.'

Finding a parking space near the main buildings of the ski resort, the two women handed over their vouchers to receive another meal featuring dumplings.

Georgia felt suddenly weary.

'I feel like I've been on a full shift already,' she told Kate. 'And we're only a third of our way through the competition. At least we get a break after this. I'm going to try and catch a nap.'

After they'd eaten, they went outside into the sunshine and found a grassy patch to lie on that was shaded by a huge tree. Georgia closed her eyes and hoped that Kate would think she had fallen asleep.

She just needed a little quiet time and maybe she could stop the unsettling thoughts that were only a distraction to why she was really here and then she could focus completely on winning this competition.

Childhood memories of the trauma of being forcibly taken from her mother, the intervention of child protection services and then being moved from one town to another until her father's death had finally freed them from the threat that had never gone away but were of no help to her concentration.

Stupid dreams of finding 'the one', like Kate still had, were just as useless.

The plan of launching her new future as a single parent by choosing her baby daddy at this competition were well and truly being laid to rest.

Because, if she had the choice, she wouldn't be able to choose anyone other than Matteo?

And he would end up finding out, wouldn't he? He was best friends with *her* best friend's friend and secrets had a nasty tendency to get revealed eventually.

Besides…she liked him.

She *really* liked him. Too much to consider the kind of deception that would end up haunting her for ever.

Her breath escaped in a small sigh as she turned her mind back to the tasks they had already completed today. The baby resuscitation. All those little scamps creating havoc in the schoolroom.

And thinking about those children produced an idea that Georgia hadn't ever considered before.

Perhaps she didn't actually need to have a baby herself. There were always children who needed adoption or fostering. Children who were having to live with the kind of trauma she knew about all too well.

She'd be good at that.

With another long, outward breath, Georgia relaxed into the companionable silence she was sharing with Kate.

Yes. That was an idea that merited a lot more thought in the near future. When this competition was over.

CHAPTER THREE

IT WAS ALL over bar the shouting.

All tasks had been completed and the rest of the twenty-four-hour period after the lunch break had been jam packed with challenges and excitement.

The bus-crash scenario where they'd needed to triage so many injured people, including the woman who was trapped and losing a dangerous amount of blood. They'd dealt with a cardiac arrest and a young man having a stroke, whose acting had been superb. Even as Georgia had been asking her initial questions, his speech had become slurred and his face had started to droop on one side. The impressively set up scenario of a mass shooting incident in the last couple of hours had been responsible for finally using up any remaining ounce of her energy.

Skipping breakfast, she and Kate had gone to

their room to grab a few hours' sleep but it hadn't been enough. When the alarm sounded to remind them it was time to go to the competition debrief, Georgia couldn't drag herself out of bed.

'You go,' she mumbled. 'Tell me all about it later.'

The extra sleep had been exactly what she'd needed. By the time the competitors gathered in the town square for the prize-giving ceremony, Georgia was refreshed and ready for anything. Standing in the crowd beside Matteo was adding considerably to the anticipation. More than once, she found her gaze caught by his as she glanced up and their eye contact was a conversation all in itself.

A reminder of a conversation anyway.

'I intend to win.'

'So do I.'

'Do you always get what you want, Georgie?'

'Not always...'

But her heart skipped a beat as the announcement became imminent for their section of the competition.

'And the winner is… *Scotland*…'

There was a split second as Georgia sucked in an astonished breath where she was still locked in a moment of that silent communication with Matteo and she saw something change in that gaze.

He was impressed with her.

More than that. He had to be disappointed that he and Luke hadn't won but she could swear he actually looked *proud* of her and, in that instant, that meant more than anything else could have.

She wanted to be the person that this man was proud of.

Because it made her feel as if she was a better person than she'd ever been before.

But then her lungs were full of air, and happiness laced with her own pride tipped into something that had to be let out, and Georgia emitted a rather unprofessional squeal of delight, threw her arms around Kate and squeezed her best friend as hard as she could.

Even then, in that moment of pure joy, she was aware of a longing to feel Matteo's arms around her in a hug like this but there was no time for that. They had to weave their way through the sea of people and applause, to make their way to the stage and receive their trophy. The pace, and the excitement, didn't stop there either.

After the prize-giving came the convoy that was the highlight of this ceremony, where every ambulance and Jeep or makeshift emergency response vehicle put their lights and sirens on and drove through all the surrounding villages, throwing toys and sweets to the crowds of children lining the roads to enjoy the spectacle.

Georgia recognised the cute little boy from the schoolroom scenario and leaned further out of the window as they sped past to make sure her gifts landed as close as possible to his outstretched hands. When he caught the soft toy bear in a kilt that had been on the front of their car, amidst a shower of boiled sweets in the colours of the Scottish flag, she let out a whoop of satisfaction.

Matteo, who was driving, turned his head with a frown of disapproval at the danger she was putting herself in, but he was laughing at the same time.

He knew exactly how much pleasure she was getting by pushing both the limits of safety and the rules for this traditional convoy that, astonishingly, she'd just had to remind Kate of—no alcohol, no speeding and no leaning out of vehicles. It seemed that Kate was a little drunk on adventure, possibly for the first time in her life, but Georgia knew that Matteo was as addicted to this kind of adrenaline rush as she was.

Sharing that kind of personality trait would have given her an instant connection with anyone but there was more to it as far as Matteo was concerned. Not that she wanted to think about that right now. She just wanted to enjoy the delicious sound of his laughter. And his voice with that fabulous accent. And the fact that she could make the most of it all for the next few hours as all the competitors and their supporters, the officials and army of volunteers for this competition were treated to an evening of food and wine and dancing.

It was Matteo who brought a chilled bottle of champagne to the table that Georgia and Kate were sitting at, having loaded plates with offerings from one of the many barbecues being used. The long, rustic table was crowded with their new friends from places like New Zealand and Croatia and there was already a generous supply of drinks available, but that bottle of champagne instantly became the star.

Like Matteo…

He sat opposite Georgia and winked at her. 'I hadn't forgotten,' he said softly. 'You have a taste for champagne, yes?'

'Mmm…'

So this offering was a gift just for her, because he'd remembered what she liked?

Something inside Georgia was melting but she tried very hard to stop the process. Nobody was this perfect—it just wasn't humanly possible.

'So who thinks they'll do this again?' Luke asked after Matteo handed her a brimming plastic cup and filled one for himself.

'Me,' she responded instantly.

'Me,' Matteo said at exactly the same moment.

Grinning, they both raised their cups and touched them together in a toast. Their gazes touched at the same time and that melting process suddenly accelerated.

The sense of connection that was there between them was mind-blowing. It was way more than a shared love of adventure. More than anything that could be encompassed by mere physical attraction. For a heartbeat, and then another, it seemed that she and Matteo were in a space that nobody but the two of them could ever inhabit.

A dangerous space. The kind of fantasy planet that came into being when you fell head over heels in love with someone. An orbit that could only last until it got annihilated by an inevitable meteorite of discovering how wrong you'd been.

But…maybe it was possible to *visit* that planet. Just for a little while. A few hours?

The longing to do that was overpowering.

This had nothing to do with that crazy plan. This was simply the force of attraction for someone who had unexpectedly stepped into her life—and who would step out of it again very soon.

Someone with whom she felt a connection like nothing she had ever experienced before.

What would it be like to get even closer to this irresistible man?

Dave, the New Zealander, was saying something about how expensive it would be for them to come back to do the competition again but Georgia wasn't listening.

The prospect of getting *really* close to Matteo was both the most exhilarating thing ever and a bit scary. Georgia was playing with fire here, and she knew it.

At least the reminder that there were other people around them forced her to break the eye contact with Matteo but she knew the damage—if that's what it was—had already been done.

He was as aware of her as she was of him for the rest of that dinner and she knew he was watching her when she dragged Kate onto the dance floor when the lights dimmed and the live band launched into some rock and roll. It was a general invitation for everybody to start letting their hair down and enjoy themselves. It was also a private invitation for Matteo to cut in and claim her as a dance partner.

It took only a minute or two and there it was. An outstretched hand and a smile that melted her heart all over again.

The fact that they were surrounded by other people and the noise level was deafening only seemed to enhance the effect of his skin touching hers for the first time.

It was only his fingers catching hers, sending her into a twirl that took her away from Kate and towards a less densely populated part of the dance floor, but Georgia could feel the power of that touch sending a current into every cell of her body.

Circuits were being fried so that she couldn't seem to catch a coherent thought. Physical sensations, emotions, words—even the sounds, scents and colours around her were blurring into something that was too big to comprehend, let alone analyse. There were memories woven into whatever was happening, too. And desires.

Everything she had ever wanted, or could want, appeared to be within reach every time she was in contact with this man's skin. The bass notes of the music they were dancing to were a drumbeat, urging her towards…something.

Towards *this*… The look in Matteo's eyes when he tugged her off the dance floor and into a quieter corner past the doors.

As he bent his head to kiss her for the very first time…

If her brain was sending any warning that going any further could be risky, it was nothing more than a barely heard whisper amidst a roaring cacophony of desire. So easy to dismiss because it was insignificant. It didn't matter. Nothing else mattered.

Nothing else even existed…

Dancing with Georgia was like playing with light.

With fire…

The sparkle in her eyes and the shards of gold in her hair as those curls bounced and swung through shadows and into the gleam of the spotlights over the dance floor.

The way his skin burned whenever it touched hers.

He had never wanted a woman as much as he wanted Georgia Bennett right now.

He had to kiss her.

Nothing more, he warned himself as he led her away from the dance floor. This was too special to ruin by moving too fast. This was the beginning of something that made this first night together far too important to enjoy as nothing more than a casual sexual encounter.

But he had to kiss her. To find out whether the touch of her lips—the *taste* of her—could actually be as incredible as he believed it could be.

And, *Dio mio*, it was even more than he had believed was possible.

He had found the woman of his dreams. Gorgeous and clever enough to keep him on his toes. Someone with a passion for the same things in life. A body that was perfect, with just the right curves in all the right places. A combination that coalesced into a response to his own that was taking him somewhere he'd never been before.

In love…

Head-over-heels, crazily in love…

'Ti desidero,' he murmured, when he could finally lift his lips from hers enough to form any words. *'Così tanto.'*

It was safe to say how much he wanted her, wasn't it? She hadn't given any hint that she could understand his native language.

But maybe the language of love was universal and it was the tone that said it all, because Georgia's eyes were huge in this dark corner and they were telling him that she knew exactly what he was saying.

'Me, too,' she whispered.

He could feel the way she drew in a quick breath because his hands were still on her ribcage, his hands cradling the delicious weight of her breasts.

She used that breath to form some more words. 'My room or yours?'

For a heartbeat, Matteo froze, and that in itself was shocking. At any point in his life before this, he wouldn't have hesitated in accepting such an invitation from a beautiful woman. Sex was one of life's greatest pleasures after all.

But this was different.

Georgia was different.

And this…connection between them was so new. So beautiful but also fragile.

What if she thought he was only interested in the sex? That it meant nothing more than that?

Or what if he rejected the offer and she disappeared because she thought he *wasn't* interested?

He couldn't think straight. And then he saw the tip of Georgia's tongue appear and trace the outline of her bottom lip.

He could barely muster any words in Italian, let alone English.

'I haven't got… I mean it might not be…safe…'

He could feel the movement of her body between his hands as she pressed herself closer. She lifted her face, inviting him to kiss her again.

'It's safe,' she said softly, her eyelids lowering to shutter her gaze. 'I promise.'

A promise was a vow and Matteo let his eyes drift shut as he sank into the astonishing way her lips responded to his. The touch of her tongue sealed his fate. He trusted her.

How could he not trust the woman he knew he was destined to marry?

The grand, if half-baked, plan of finding someone suitable to father her child had not even been a consideration when Georgia had made that promise to Matteo that this was safe.

The fact that she'd lied to him by inferring that she was on the Pill or in a safe part of her cycle had also been dismissed as unimportant as she allowed herself to be swept away on this tidal wave of pure desire.

Okay, maybe that whisper of warning had returned to try and sneak past the breath-stealing anticipation as she led Matteo to her bedroom in the accommodation block but it had been a short walk and all it had needed to send any doubts into oblivion had been the look in Matteo's eyes and the touch of his fingers as he began to unbutton her shirt. Her knees almost buckled as he bent his head to kiss the curve of her breasts just before he undid the clasp of her bra and somehow tipping her head back in ecstasy had the same effect on the rest of her body and there they were—squashed onto the narrow confines of her single bed.

The size of that bed made it so much harder to shed the rest of their clothing but it didn't seem to matter. Any awkwardness dissolved under low peals of laughter, of pausing to share another passionate kiss. Of moving to make things easier that only brought new areas of their skin into contact. The only light came from the moon beyond an unshaded window but Georgia didn't need to use her eyes to discover that Matteo's body was as perfect as she had suspected. She only needed her fingers and her lips and sometimes her tongue to explore the planes of hard muscle, the soft fur of masculine hair and the exquisitely tender skin in secret places.

She only needed her own skin to experience the power in his hands but it was her heart that registered the astonishing gentleness with which that power was being harnessed.

Georgia had never been made love to like this. Carried to a place of such a mind-blowing release that it was inevitable that the roller-coaster would dip in its aftermath. Even so, it was a bit of a shock to find it so hard to swallow past a painful constriction in her throat as she lay in Matteo's arms, feeling the thump of his heartbeat finally returning to a normal level.

If she had been a crying type—which she certainly wasn't—she would have tears trickling down her face by now, wouldn't she?

It was a shock, too, to realise how hard it was going to be to walk away from this man.

She'd just given Matteo more than her body. Right now, her brain was fighting to retrieve her heart.

'I want to see you again,' Matteo murmured. 'Soon…'

Georgia turned her head so that she couldn't get undone by those eyes. She wanted to see him again soon as well. So much that it scared her.

'You live in Italy,' she reminded him. 'Scotland is a long way away.'

'Nessun problema.' He was smiling. 'I can find a way. I'm ready for new adventures. Scotland must be a very exciting place to work on rescue helicopters, yes? Lots of mountain work?'

Oh...*help*... How amazing would that be? To have Matteo living and working in Scotland? To be with him again, like *this*...

Again and again. To forge a relationship that could last the rest of their lives?

She'd done it again, hadn't she? Fallen in love at the drop of a hat and now she was dreaming of that little church and the house with a picket fence and a whole tribe of adorable children.

She couldn't do this.

She'd *promised* herself she would never be stupid enough to do this again. And she'd meant it.

The sliver of fear already in existence gathered force and shivered its way down her spine. There was a hint of anger there as well, that she'd allowed herself to let things go this far.

Not just the falling-in-love kind of far. She'd taken a huge risk in having unprotected sex.

Using Matteo as a sperm donor hadn't even crossed her mind when she had been swept away by this overwhelming chemistry. When she'd told him it was safe, it had been because she had somehow convinced herself that she was in a safe part of her cycle.

She had to be, because she hadn't been able to fight a desire like nothing she'd ever experienced before.

However long the odds were, however, the possibility was there. And if she hadn't won that spin of the pregnancy roulette wheel, there would be consequences she didn't want to have to think about.

What she could think about were the consequences of imagining that this initial head-rush of falling in love could last and become something permanent and trustworthy.

She knew how unlikely that was.

She knew how gutting it was when the dreams crashed and burned.

Georgia had just had one perfect night. The best thing she could do would be to keep it like that. Bottle it into a memory that would never get tarnished.

'I can't do that,' she heard herself whisper, her words strained with the effort of releasing them.

She felt the subtle shift of Matteo's body. The birth of a tension that encompassed bewilderment and something else. Something darker.

'Why not? I… I thought we had something special here, *cara*.'

'We do.' There was a gap between them now but that couldn't entirely explain the chill she could feel. 'But that's just it. This is *here*. Anywhere else would be…impossible.'

She had to meet the intense gaze she could feel on her face. Even in this dim light she could see the expression in those dark eyes.

She was hurting him and she hated herself for that.

Enough that she could change her mind and

break her vow? Take the risk that her heart was insisting would be worth it this time?

She actually parted her lips to tell him that but she didn't get the chance to speak.

Matteo was rolling away from her. Getting to his feet and starting to gather his clothes.

'So this was just a one-night stand for you?' He had dragged on his underwear and now his trousers.

The slip in his excellent English was poignant enough to make Georgia catch her bottom lip with her teeth. To generate the prickle that warned of tears she would never allow to fall.

Matteo didn't bother doing up his belt. He was pushing his arms through the sleeves of his shirt with jerky movements.

'There's someone else, isn't there?' He sounded angry now. 'Someone in Scotland? You're *cheating* on someone?'

Oh, how was it possible for one word to convey such ultimate disgust?

Georgia closed her eyes.

She remembered the conversation over drinks

that first night. When Kate had been shocked to discover not only that Luke was no longer married but that his best friend had never known his ex-wife's name and only referred to her as 'the cheating cow'?

She could hear Matteo's words echoing in the back of her mind.

'If someone cheated on me or lied to me like that, I would never let her name pass my lips again...'

This was it. The easy way out. No further excuses would have to be found and Matteo's attitude to both cheating and lying would ensure that he didn't try to contact her again. He believed he'd been used for no more than a bit of fun. Worse, fun at someone else's expense. Someone who would possibly be devastated if they found out.

She knew that Matteo had been aware of the same level of connection she'd discovered with him so she couldn't blame him for being so angry. If the situation were reversed she would feel exactly the same way.

Getting her next word out was going to be the hardest thing she'd ever done.

She couldn't do it, in fact. All she could manage was a single nod of her head and that felt like an acknowledgement of how justified Matteo was to be reacting like this but, of course, it was interpreted as a confirmation of his accusation that she was cheating on a boyfriend back home.

And, maybe, the sane corner of Georgia's brain had intended it to be taken that way.

As she closed her eyes, she saw Matteo swoop on his shoes and socks but she knew he hadn't bothered to put them on.

Because she heard the door of her room slam shut only seconds later.

CHAPTER FOUR

IT WAS OFTEN the case that normal life could seem dull in the aftermath of an overseas holiday or a challenging adventure.

And Georgia Bennett had combined both of those into the few days of the Rally Rakovi international medical rescue competition. It had been the most extraordinary few days of her life and it was no surprise that she felt flat for a while after getting home.

But surely this heavy cloud of fatigue laced with waves of something that bordered on misery at frequent intervals should have worn off by now?

It had been *weeks*…

Enough time for the glory of arriving home as a winner and impressing all her colleagues at the

Edinburgh Emergency Response Centre to have worn off.

Enough time to have had evidence that she been right to assume she had been in a safe part of her cycle when she'd slept with Matteo. That, even if she'd gone further down that unwise path of hoping to get pregnant by someone she would never have to see again, a one-off encounter would have been a disappointing failure.

And it was a huge relief. Of course it was.

She wasn't disappointed because she hadn't expected anything different. She had, in fact, been waiting for her period to start with an acute anticipation of the relief that it would bring.

It would be a line being drawn under that very brief chapter in her life. It would make it so much easier to put it all behind her, neatly packaged in a memory box that could be labelled 'The Rally'. Or, probably more accurately, 'Matteo'.

Georgia would, at last, be able to embrace life and the job she was so passionate about with all the enthusiasm and determination that was so much a part of who she was.

But there had been a note of, not disappointment, but sadness to be found amidst that wash of relief. She had taken a risk after all, and so there'd been that small chance that she could have conceived. Her brain might be telling her in no uncertain terms that it was a good thing she wasn't but her body—and her heart—were whispering a reminder of how much she wanted to become a mother. That, if it had happened, it would have been a genuine accident so she could have avoided the guilt of knowing she had done something she knew would have been so wrong.

As a final kicker, it almost felt as if someone or something in the cosmos was mocking the fact that she had stepped back, however briefly, into that fantasy planet of true love and happy-ever-afters. Of holding her own baby in her arms for the first time and feeling like her heart would burst from the joy of it.

She was putting a brave face on it, of course, and she was confident that nobody had guessed the internal struggle she was grappling with.

Certainly not her crew partner, Sean, whose

face brightened with the priority call that was coming through on their pagers.

'*Yes*…a cardiac arrest. Finally—we get to save a life today. Come on, champ.'

It had been her new nickname on station ever since she had come back with the trophy that was now proudly on display in the staffroom. Every paramedic who worked here and even the doctors and other medical professionals she encountered during her working hours had wanted details about the competition. A description of how it all worked, of what the scenarios had involved and about the level of skill other competitors had displayed.

She'd told them everything they'd wanted to know. Encouraged them to think about entering themselves for a 'once in a lifetime' experience. The one thing she never mentioned, however, was what had left the most lasting personal impression.

Matteo Martini.

Georgia followed Sean at a run, slamming the passenger door of the ambulance and reaching for her safety belt as the garage doors came up and Sean put his foot down on the accelerator, flicking on the lights and siren the moment they exited the station gates.

Thank goodness the interest in the competition had finally worn off. She'd spent far more time than was healthy reliving every moment she had had with Matteo anyway. Every conversation, every glance, every touch. Being reminded of him every time she had talked about the rally to people who had no idea how much of an impact it had had on her had been a form of emotional torture.

It was still all bottled up inside her and she had no idea how to deal with it.

She couldn't even tell Kate about it, which had always been her go-to therapy for any emotional woes because Kate was more than a little starry-eyed about reconnecting with her friend from medical school and Luke was Matteo's best friend and it was all...complicated. Just a bit of mess, really.

Thrown into her seatbelt as Sean braked behind

a slow car that seemed unaware of the noise of the siren and flashing lights was a helpful distraction. The blast he gave on the air horn to order the car to pull over and let them through the traffic was enough to tickle her adrenaline levels and she actually laughed as the ambulance swerved and even mounted the kerb briefly to get past the obstruction.

Sean sent a grin sideways.

Her favourite crew partner was enjoying this as much as she was. Relatively new to their station, Sean had become instantly popular. Tall, good looking and with a very cute Irish accent, he was particularly popular with his female colleagues and a month or two ago Georgia might have been interested herself, despite having sworn off the search for a long-term relationship in the wake of that crushing break-up with Rick.

But not now.

She liked him. And she loved working with him but as far as anything more was concerned, she couldn't summon even a flicker of interest.

Because he wasn't Matteo Martini?

Yeah... The bar had been reset at an impossibly high level, hadn't it? Which was a good thing, Georgia told herself, because she didn't want to go there. She didn't want to get lured back into a situation where the odds of it ending well, as in not ending at all, were sadly virtually non-existent in her experience. And she was at risk because she fell in love too easily.

Perhaps the most astonishing thing she'd learned about herself during those intense few days of the competition was that she was actually capable of falling in love at first sight...

'Next on the right,' she called. 'And then second on the left. ETA two minutes.'

'Roger. Hold onto your hat. And it's your turn to lead.'

With a nod, Georgia focussed on what lay immediately ahead. It would be a long shot, saving someone who had been found in cardiac arrest, given that it had been an unwitnessed collapse so they didn't know when it had happened, or whether effective bystander CPR was currently being performed, but she would give the effort everything she had.

Probably a little bit more, even, because this was her life and she wanted to love it again with the same passion she'd had before she'd gone to that damn competition.

The battle hadn't been won.

The resuscitation effort had been protracted, messy and, in the end, very sad. The victim had only been in his early fifties and his first grandchild was due to be born next week. His wife had been distraught and then his pregnant daughter had arrived at the house as they had been clearing away their gear and waiting for the doctor to come and sign the death certificate.

Georgia was not going to allow herself to dwell on this case, however. If she did, she knew she would sink even further into a space she knew was there but didn't recognise.

A dark space where the hovering cloud of bone-deep fatigue with those shards of misery would come down and block out any remaining light in her life. Where she might start to feel so sorry for herself that it would become too hard to pick herself up and make things better.

It wasn't going to happen.

Georgia Bennett had faced worse things than this in her life and she had learned that she could not only beat them, she could become stronger.

Her share of the best things in life were just around the corner.

Maybe she couldn't see exactly where that corner was just yet but if she didn't stop moving forward, she would never find it.

So she put the distressing end to her shift firmly into the part of her brain reserved for work hours and made every effort to enjoy being home. She loved this little stone cottage that she shared with Kate, with its pretty garden and cosy kitchen and the steep, narrow staircase that led to their attic bedrooms.

She loved Kate's company, too. And her cooking. It was no hardship to tackle the dishes after eating the dinner that her flatmate had prepared tonight and their conversation offered an opportunity to think of someone other than herself for a while.

It was way past time that Kate and Luke got together—the way they had promised they would when they were both back in Scotland. How good would it be if she could look back on that competition and realise that it had been the catalyst for something amazing instead of the dark cloud that was making life so much less bright for herself? If something wonderful came from the interest she knew that Kate had in Luke?

'Make it happen,' she urged Kate. 'You never know—it could change your life.'

When they went into the sitting room to finish their evening by relaxing in front of the television and Kate discovered a text from Luke on her phone, Georgia was dismayed to find herself feeling…envious?

How would she feel if she found a text from Matteo on *her* phone?

It wasn't beyond the realms of possibility, was it? He could easily get access to her phone number by asking Luke to get it from Kate.

She could get *his* number by reversing the route.

And say what? Admit that there was no boy-friend that had been waiting for her back in Scot-land so she hadn't been cheating on anyone?

By doing that, she would be admitting that she'd lied to him. Only by omission, but Geor-gia knew instinctively that a boundary like that would mean nothing to Matteo. Playing by the rules and, above all, being honest was an un-shakeable foundation for the character that made him who he was.

Someone genuine. Trustworthy.

Luke was genuine, too, but Kate was shaking her head over a proposed date that wasn't going to fit with her hospital shifts. Saying that maybe it was never meant to happen.

'Don't be ridiculous.' Georgia was in danger of losing patience. 'What were the odds of you two meeting up again on a mountaintop in the Czech Republic? It was totally meant to happen.'

Kate's smile was endearingly shy. 'It was cer-tainly unexpected.'

And then her smile widened. 'And it was you

who had the mad idea of hooking up with someone while we were there. It was the last thing I was planning on doing.'

Oh… God…talking about that crazy plan she'd had for the competition was the last thing Georgia wanted to do. Trying to dismiss this conversational track, Georgia shrugged and turned away.

'I'm not the only one who's been a bit quiet since we got back. What aren't you talking about?'

'Nothing.' She thought she'd managed a tone light enough to squash any suspicions but it didn't seem to work. She could feel Kate staring at her back.

'You never did tell me where you disappeared to for so long during that party.'

Georgia froze.

'Oh, my God,' Kate said. 'You *did* hook up with somebody. And you never told me?'

'Wasn't much to tell.' Georgia's forced the words out. 'I'd rather forget about it.'

But Kate didn't take the hint. 'It can't have been Matteo,' she said, 'because I saw him and asked if he knew where you were and he said he had no idea.'

Oh, help… Kate must have seen him shortly after he'd slammed the door and stormed off after making love to her. Had Kate been aware of how angry he'd been? Had Matteo said anything to Luke that might make this whole mess even messier in the near future?

There was no point crossing that bridge until it became unavoidable but that meant that Georgia had to kill this conversation. Now. She glared at her friend.

'Why would it have been Matteo?'

'Oh, I don't know… Because he was gorgeous maybe? Or because you two seemed to be getting on incredibly well?'

Georgia put considerable effort into a dismissive shrug. 'I guess some people aren't okay with casual sex. I don't think I am any more either. It wasn't my best idea, was it?' She reached for the television remote. 'Let's see if there's something worth watching, shall we?'

The silence between them was odd. Georgia

hated that she was deceiving Kate but she couldn't tell her the truth, could she?

If Kate had any inkling how she felt about Matteo, she would try and fix things, wouldn't she? Like Georgia had been trying to fix things between Kate and Luke by encouraging her to text him?

Kate might think she was doing the right thing by enlisting Luke's assistance. And then Matteo would find out and it would just make everything messier. Because he wouldn't want to know.

He wouldn't want her name to even pass his lips because she had lied to him.

Besides…she wanted to stop thinking about it. To stop the ongoing battle between her head and her heart about whether it could be worth taking the kind of risk that another relationship represented.

To move on from thinking that she'd made a mistake that could never be fixed.

And she was *so* tired…

Kate finally seemed to pick up the vibe. She

sat on the couch beside Georgia and gave her a quick hug.

'It's in the past now,' she said. 'And, yeah…it wasn't your best idea but you'll know not to do it again.'

Wasn't that the truth?

She'd never have the chance to do it again.

'Are you okay? Really?'

Georgia nodded, hugging her back. 'I'm fine. *Really.*'

'Want a coffee?'

The wave of nausea the idea of coffee produced was weird. She must be a lot more tired than she'd realised.

'No.' Georgia shook her head, closing her eyes and swallowing hard in the hope that her stomach would settle quickly. 'Let's just chill out and watch some telly.'

After an adrenaline-filled day of big-city emergency response, there was nothing better than chilling with an old mate and an icy-cold beer.

And today had been one to remember. A huge

pile-up on one of the motorways just outside Milan with critically injured people who'd needed to get to a major trauma facility in less time than any ambulance was capable of. They'd had to land their helicopter on the motorway, more than once, in a tight space that the police had managed to create in the middle of a traffic jam that would be making national headlines tomorrow.

Matteo Martini leaned back into the body-shaped dent on his favourite couch, his laptop on his knees, thoroughly enjoying one of his regular catch-ups via Skype with Luke. They'd just had a very interesting conversation about 4D magnetic resonance imaging and the implications that such an advance in technology could give the world of medicine.

And then the conversation got more personal.

'What's happening in your life?' Luke asked.

Matteo shrugged. 'Nothing exciting. Same old.'

'How did the date work out last week? With… um…what was her name again? That nurse?'

'Marcella.' Matteo wasn't proud of the fact that

it was an effort to remember. 'It was okay. I think she only wanted my body.'

Luke laughed. 'Lucky you.'

Yeah… It had been a welcome release after several weeks of abstinence.

But it had also been disappointing because that was all it had been.

Because she hadn't been Georgia Bennett?

No… He wasn't going to think about her. He had dismissed her from his life in the instant he'd learned that she'd been cheating on someone to be with him.

He was still angry.

Still felt cheated on himself, in fact.

No. It was more than that.

He had given away a piece of his heart.

And he wanted it back, dammit.

He was only half listening to Luke telling him how good things were between him and Kate now. About the new adventures they were sharing. He was happy for his friend, he really was. It was just unfortunate that the new woman in his life was such close friends with the woman Matteo was determined to forget.

A bubble of something he couldn't control put her name on his lips. Maybe it was the mention of having gone out dancing because it dragged him back to that time on the dance floor in Rakovi. To the time when he'd been so sure that he'd found the only woman in the world who he wanted to spend the rest of his life with.

'Did Georgia go too?' He had to fight to keep any hint of bitterness from his tone. 'And her... her boyfriend? Are you double dating?'

Thinking about the man who was lucky enough to have Georgia in his life created a tightness in his chest that made it noticeably more difficult to suck in a new breath.

When some of that initial anger had burned off, he'd actually thought of trying to contact Georgia. Of getting her number from Luke, via Kate.

But then what?

Would he knowingly set out to break an existing relationship?

Would he want to be with a woman who would leave someone else for him?

Of course not. You'd spend the rest of your life with the suspicion that the person you were devoting your life to was capable of cheating on and abandoning you if a better prospect came along.

'No.' Luke was sounding a little puzzled. 'I haven't seen Georgia since Kate and I have been together. We meet somewhere. Or Kate comes to my place.'

'Why don't you go to hers?'

'I don't know.' Luke frowned. 'I guess because she hasn't suggested it yet.'

'Maybe Georgia disapproves.'

'Why would she do that?'

'Dunno.' Matteo shrugged again. 'She's got some funny ideas, that one.'

'I thought you liked her.' Luke was still frowning.

Like…

What an insipid word. It wasn't even on the same verbal planet as something that could begin to describe the feelings Georgia had evoked.

Even *love* didn't quite encompass the sense of promise and potential fulfilment that that connection had provided.

That connection that should never have happened because it had resulted in someone being cheated on.

'I thought I did, too,' he muttered. 'Shows how wrong you can be about some people, I guess.' He needed to stop talking about Georgia. It certainly wasn't helping his determined effort to stop even thinking about her. 'Hey, man. I'd better go. Early shift tomorrow.'

'No worries. Let's do it again next week.'

Matteo grinned back. 'We might be doing it for real before long. Don't forget you can't get married unless I'm your best man.'

He stared at a blank screen for a long moment when the call had ended.

Marriage…

Children. A family of his very own. He'd always known that was going to be the very best part of his future. It had been no more than a pleasant daydream all through his twenties because he'd known he had plenty of time to play. To do all the things that a devoted father and family man would never dream of doing.

Besides, he'd needed to play the field to make sure he found the perfect woman to share his life with. Because there would only ever be one woman he would marry and she wasn't just going to be his wife. She was going to be the mother of his children.

How had all those years slipped past so quickly? He'd begun to feel the clock ticking as he'd hit his early thirties and he *had* begun to take his relationships more seriously—when his hectic work hours had allowed, that was. He'd known that his dream of being a father instead of merely an uncle wasn't going to happen all by itself. He had to make it happen.

And he had truly believed, just for the tiny blink of time that that competition had provided, that he had found the person he could make it happen *with*.

But now that dream seemed further away than it had ever been and the reality check was laced with doubts. Sadness even. Maybe it wouldn't even be as good as he'd believed it would be.

Because the woman he married was not going to be Georgia Bennett.

'It's just a bug or something, Sean. I'm fine. Unlock the door and let's get back to station. I want to go home.'

'Nope.' Georgia's partner leaned against the back of the ambulance. 'I'm not going anywhere until you go and get checked out. You've been off colour for way too long. You're tired all the time and you turned your nose up at one of Nico's kebabs today. You have to be sick not to want the best kebab ever.'

'I wasn't hungry, that's all.'

'You're off colour. You've been off colour for weeks. Get back into ED and find a nice doctor. It's quiet. Get a blood test or something.'

'That would take ages. We're off duty. It's time to go home.'

'Exactly. We've got all the time in the world. I'm going to let them know we'll be delayed getting the truck back to station and then I'm going to get coffee and chat up some nurses. Page me when you're done.'

And Sean walked off, the keys to the ambulance still in his pocket.

Fifteen minutes later and Georgia was sitting in the office of Kathryn—one of the emergency department consultants who'd been only too happy to talk to her.

'The bloods won't be back for a few minutes yet, Georgie.' Her gaze was thoughtful. 'Are you sure there's no possibility of you being pregnant?'

'I'm sure.' But Georgia bit her lip. 'I mean, *theoretically* there is. I did have unprotected sex a while back but I haven't missed a period.'

'And your periods have been normal?'

The overwhelming memory was the anticipated relief at the first sign of that period, with that disturbing aftertaste of sadness, but what had the next day been like? Georgia thought harder.

'Lighter than normal, I guess. Especially the last one.'

Kathryn nodded. 'I think we might go and borrow the portable ultrasound while we're waiting for those bloods.'

Georgia couldn't identify the emotion that seemed to be gathering somewhere deep inside her gut.

Horror...or hope?

'You've heard of decidual bleeding, haven't you?' The consultant was leading her into a cubicle and whisking the curtain shut behind them. She carried on speaking as Georgia got onto the bed and unbuttoned her uniform trousers. 'Twenty to thirty percent of women will have some type of bleeding in the first trimester. It's not uncommon for spotting or light bleeding to carry on into the second or even third trimesters.'

'Yeah... I've heard of it.' The gel was cold against the skin of her abdomen.

'It's due to hormones being a bit out of whack. More common in the early days, before the lining of the uterus has completely attached to the placenta. In most cases, it's not thought to be a threat to the baby.' Kathryn was staring at the screen of the ultrasound machine as she angled the probe.

There was silence for a long moment. Too long for Georgia to keep holding her breath.

'Oh, my God…' she whispered. 'You can see something, can't you? I *am* pregnant?'

The sideways glance she received was cautious. 'How would you feel about that?'

'Um…'

Unidentifiable emotions were roiling now. Fear and excitement. Memories of how strong that desire to have a baby had been. Strong enough to have made her come up with the plan that the international competition was the perfect place to find the father of her longed-for baby.

An intense flashback to how it had felt being with Matteo. Being touched by his hands and lips.

That twist of sadness that fate hadn't stepped in to override her decision that she couldn't possibly go through with the plan.

'I think… I think I would be very happy about that.'

'Hmm...' Kathryn angled the screen so that Georgia could see the image. Not that she could recognise the blobs amongst the grainy black and white shapes but she could see something moving rhythmically. The beat of a tiny heart...

No...wait...

Time seemed to be standing still as her startled gaze caught the doctor's steady one.

'So...' Kathryn's question was somewhat tentative. 'You're going to be twice as happy to know that you're pregnant with twins?'

CHAPTER FIVE

IT COULDN'T REMAIN a secret.

If it was a singleton pregnancy, she could probably have kept her situation private for months and passed off any new roundness in her belly and breasts as a bit of weight gain due to being slack with her healthy eating or exercise regime. But she had two babies growing inside her belly.

Two...

In a very short space of time—weeks at the most—Georgia knew that the changes in her body were going to be blindingly obvious to the whole world.

So she might as well spill the beans now, yes?

No.

One look at the puzzled frown on Sean's face as she re-joined her colleague, who had been waiting patiently for more than an hour, was enough to change her mind. The news would be like throwing a large stone into a pond. There were going to be big ripples that would affect other people as well. She could be taken off the road sooner rather than later and probably given some boring tasks that involved a lot of paperwork or time in storerooms. She would lose the joy of working with Sean on the road and the distraction that the variety and challenges of every job could provide. Being consigned to light duties would give her far too much time to think. About the future.

About the father of her babies…

This was a multiple pregnancy that carried higher risks for complications, she reminded herself, and she wasn't even that close to the end of her first trimester. It might be unwise to throw that rock before it was absolutely necessary.

'What is it?' Sean demanded.

'Nothing,' Georgia told him airily. 'I'm fine. Let's go home.'

Sean started the ambulance a minute or two later but his sideways glance was suspicious.

'I don't believe you.'

'I'm not sick, Sean.' It was easy to sound convincing. Pregnancy wasn't an illness. It was a perfectly normal state for a woman's body to be in.

'You look…different.'

'Do I?'

'Yeah…' It took another couple of searching glances before Sean could identify what was puzzling him. 'You look… I dunno…like you thought you had a terminal illness and you've been given the all-clear. Like you've won the lottery or something.'

Georgia's response was a bubble of laughter.

'You're right. I'd started wondering if I had some horrible disease but I haven't. I'm just…'

Pregnant.

'Just a bit rundown. I'm going to live to be a hundred years old and I'm happy.' She beamed at her partner. 'You should be happy, too. We'll be working together until we're old and grey.'

Sean laughed as well. 'I'll be grey by the time I'm thirty, working with you, champ. Don't scare me like that again.'

* * *

It was fortunate that Kate was staying with Luke tonight, Georgia decided when she arrived home. She had never needed a bit of quiet time more than she did right now.

Snatches of her conversation with Sean were still running through her mind. She had told him that she wasn't sick and it was the truth because pregnancy *was* a completely normal state for a woman's body to deal with.

Except it wasn't normal for *her*, was it?

It was… It was…

Incredible…

She was going to have a *baby*. No…*two* babies…

In a matter of months she wouldn't be simply a single mother with a baby. She'd be a mother with an entire little family.

A smile was trying to break out but there was a prickle behind her eyes that was so unfamiliar it took a moment for Georgia to recognise the imminent threat of tears.

Tears? She had learned how useless tears were when she'd been five years old and she'd only cried once since then—at her mother's funeral. Or, rather, well after the funeral, where there was nobody around to witness the evidence of weakness.

Maybe that was the reason for this current threat. If there was one person she'd want to talk to about how she was feeling right now, it would be her mother.

Closely followed by Kate, of course, but throwing her rock in that direction would be more like aiming for a minefield than a pond.

Kate would be horrified at her flagrant disregard of how to achieve what she wanted within the rules of normal social behaviour. Wanting a family was no problem, but you were supposed to at least try to do it the right way. To be careful about contraception until you believed you had found a partner in life. Preferably until after you had married that partner.

There would be endless discussions. It was more than likely that Kate could home in on fears for the future that Georgia didn't want to think about yet. Things like where she was going to live and how she would be able to cope financially. She would probably only be being a responsible friend if she pointed out that Georgia still had options at this very early stage of her pregnancy.

Even as she was still reeling at the news that Kathryn had delivered, Georgia knew that the idea of not going ahead with this pregnancy was completely unthinkable but she did need time to get used to this…this rather overwhelmingly unexpected miracle.

And it *was* a miracle.

In the end, she hadn't planned for this to happen. She hadn't set out to seduce a potentially acceptable sperm donor on the off-chance of hitting the jackpot. She had been hugely relieved that an accidental pregnancy had been avoided.

Because she'd known how complicated it could become if Kate knew the truth.

For the first time since the shocking moment when she'd seen that tiny heart beating on the ultrasound screen, Georgia felt a flash of fear.

Kate couldn't know the truth. Not about who

had fathered these babies anyway. The truth about the pregnancy would have to come out, of course. But not yet. Hopefully not until she'd had time to get all her ducks in a row and would have a convincing argument to counter any objections that Kate could come up with.

It was the eggs that did it.

Ruined any plans that Georgia was still formulating about the quiet conversation she was planning to have with Kate when she was ready.

Something about the sight of that congealed egg yolk on the white plates stacked in the sink ready to be washed, combined with the weariness of having just completed a busy night shift, and the vague nausea Georgia had been aware of for some time suddenly tipped into something far more violent. She ran towards the bathroom in the hope that she would make it as far as the toilet before her stomach turned itself inside out.

She didn't even notice that Kate had followed her until she felt the welcome touch of a damp facecloth as she finally let go of the cold, ceramic bowl of the toilet and sat back on her heels.

'I'll never eat eggs again in my life,' she groaned.

'You didn't eat any in the first place. You just looked at the plates.'

'I know…' Georgia leaned back against the wall, the facecloth pressed against her eyes. Had she really reassured Sean that she wasn't sick a couple of weeks ago? She had never felt this unwell in her life.

'Are you sick? Running a temperature?' Kate went into doctor mode, taking hold of her wrist to feel for her pulse.

'I don't think so.'

'Did you eat something dodgy on night shift? Like a kebab?'

'No.'

'Oh, my God…' After a short silence in which the sound of pennies dropping was almost audible, Kate sounded horrified. 'Are you pregnant. Georgie?'

So much for picking her own moment to share this news.

Kate's heavy sigh as she shifted to lean against the wall beside Georgia was exactly how she was feeling herself.

'When were you going to tell me?'

'When it was too late to have an argument about whether or not it was a good idea to go through with it.'

Kate's breath came out in a shocked huff. 'Did you think I'd try and persuade you to have a termination?'

Georgia took the facecloth away from her eyes. If the truth was coming out, it may as well be the whole truth. Well…not *quite* the whole truth, of course…

'Why not? You've never approved of my plan for single parenthood. You told me the whole idea was hare-brained.'

'That doesn't mean I wouldn't support you in whatever you chose to do.' There was a wobble in Kate's voice that broke Georgia's heart. It had felt so wrong keeping this a secret from her best friend and this was her punishment.

She had hurt Kate.

'I can't believe you've kept this to yourself. How pregnant *are* you?'

'About ten weeks.'

The silence was short. And shocked.

'So you did hook up with someone at the rally. I *knew* there was something you weren't telling me. Who was it?'

'It doesn't matter.'

'Of course it matters. It's your child's father. You need to know about family genetics. You'll need financial support.'

Georgia shook her head sharply enough to make her stomach try to roll again but she wasn't about to be sick. The rush of adrenaline that fear produced was enough to buy her some time.

'That's precisely the reason I did it this way. I don't want to know about the father's family. I don't want financial support. I don't want anyone interfering in any way. This is *my* baby. And it's going to stay that way.'

It *had* to stay that way.

From a dark, buried space in the back of her mind, Georgia could hear a small voice.

The small voice of a terrified child.

'Don't let them take me, Mummy. I don't want to go...'

'You're coming with us. You're my *daughter. You're going to get brought up in a decent, Godly household, not dragged up by your slut of a mother. Get in the car now and* stay *there...'*

There was pain mixed in with the terror as the car door slammed shut on the arm still reaching out in a desperate plea to the woman this man was shoving back with his other arm. She could see her mother fall to the footpath, could see the blood on the strange shape of her arm as she tumbled and then curled up on the back seat of the vehicle that was taking her away from everything she knew and loved.

Georgia squeezed her eyes shut against the agonising memory. Kate didn't know about her childhood. Nobody did. If people asked her about that scar on her arm, she told them she'd fallen off her pony one day, when she'd been out jumping every log she could find on the hills behind her country village. She'd covered the horrible reality with a fantasy of a perfect childhood so often she almost believed it herself. The only other person who'd known the real truth and could understand the fear that had poisoned so many years of her life had been her mother and she'd lost that rock in her life a long time ago.

She couldn't begin to try and explain any of this, even to her best friend. Because it was too big and she'd walled those memories off and tried to bury them for a very good reason—she didn't *want* to remember any of it.

It was inevitable that knowing she was bringing her own children into the world had prompted a backward glance at what was behind those mental walls but that was only as far as Georgia was prepared to go.

So she couldn't tell Kate why but she could make her understand that Georgia wasn't going to change her mind. She knew she was pushing her closest friend away with her vehement tone but this was self-protection.

No. It was even more important than that. She was protecting her babies.

It was a blessing that she'd stopped herself telling Kate how she felt about Matteo due to the link she had to him via Luke. Somehow, instinct had protected her babies even before she had known they existed.

It was infinitely more important that Kate never know this part of the truth because Matteo would never let his children be brought up by someone he despised.

Maybe he wouldn't be as violent as her father had been but he would be just as persistent, even if he didn't believe that he had a vengeful God on his side.

Okay, she knew that Matteo would never condone violence. That he would probably be as reasonable as any co-parent could be and he would allow her access to her babies—perhaps even shared living arrangements. But that wouldn't be enough. Life would be an endless emotional roller-coaster where the dips would consist of anxiety and loneliness and probably something as nasty as jealousy.

What if…what if Matteo found a woman he could adore instead of despise? If she became a part-time mother to *her* babies?

No. She couldn't handle that.

And she still had the power to make sure she never had to face that kind of painful disruption to her life.

'Don't ask again, Kate.' Her voice came out in a kind of hiss. 'Because I'm never going to tell you. I'm never going to tell anyone, *especially* the father. And I couldn't anyway because I don't have his address. I barely remember his name. And…oh, *God*… I'm going to be sick again…'

The morning sickness gave life an edge of misery that made the following weeks seem very long but then it began to wear off and life suddenly seemed much brighter.

On the work front, Georgia's fears of being demoted to a paper-pusher proved unfounded. Her 'light duties' were actually going to be an opportunity she'd quietly dreamed of being offered. There would be no more lifting patients or putting herself into dangerous rescue situations but she would still be able to use every skill she possessed as a paramedic. She would be challenged, in fact, because she was going to be working alone at times. Given a fully equipped SUV that had everything an ambulance had apart from any stretchers, she could be sent first to a scene to assess and start treatment. Or she could be dispatched as backup to provide the kind of interventions and drugs a less qualified crew could offer.

She was going to get all the excitement and satisfaction her job was capable of delivering, without any of the drudgery. No hard physical challenges and no long transport journeys taking perfectly stable patients to a hospital while radio traffic announced the dispatch of available crews to far more exciting-sounding calls.

Her new duties would have been more than enough to restore her zest for life as the misery of constant nausea receded but there was another bright spot that was getting steadily larger. Even before the morning sickness had kicked in, Kate and Luke had finally managed to connect and their relationship had deepened steadily. Now it seemed believable that her best friend had found exactly what she had been searching for. The One. Which was just as well because Kate had, shockingly, broken her own rules, had had unprotected sex with Luke and—astonishingly—become pregnant as easily as Georgia had herself.

Was it really only a few months ago that they were both passionate career women in their midthirties who'd been facing the prospect of futures that might not deliver the extra dimension of having a real family?

Okay, things weren't *perfect*…

Single parenthood was not really anybody's dream. For most people, it was something that you coped with when you had to. When the fairy-tale concept of family hadn't worked out for whatever reason.

But Georgia didn't see it that way.

The best times in her childhood and adolescence had been when she'd felt safe with her mother. When they'd found a new place to live and knew it could be months before her father tracked them down and made another attempt to separate them. When, at best, the police or social services would come knocking at their door and there would be court appearances or the like to deal with.

At worst, it had been when Georgia had had to start looking over her shoulder all the time in case she was being followed. Or walk home from school with the fear that she might not find her mother still alive when she got there.

Georgia knew she could do more than cope with single parenthood. Without the threat of interference, she could ensure that the lives of her children were full of joy. And love. And that they would always feel *safe*.

She also believed that everything would work out for Kate. That she and Luke had the foundations for a perfect life together.

Georgia was quite convinced about this. Until

that grey, wet day when she received the dreadful news that Kate had had an accident. That she'd been hit by a car as she'd run across a busy road.

That, while she'd been lucky enough not to receive any injuries more than a concussion, she'd lost her baby.

It was one of the hardest things Georgia had ever had to do, walking into that hospital room to bring fresh clothes and take Kate home. It felt like a giant spotlight was aimed at her belly to advertise her continuing pregnancy and rub salt into what had to be the rawest wound ever.

'I'm so, so sorry, Katy.'

But Kate brushed off her sympathy.

'It's not that big a deal, you know? I'd barely had time to get used to the idea anyway.'

And that was apparently all that Kate wanted to say about the subject. At home for the next couple of days, all she wanted to do was sleep. Georgia took time off work to watch her friend and make sure there were no signs of a more severe head injury that had been missed. That first night, she actually lay on Kate's bed beside her, waking her every so often just to check her level of responsiveness and listening to the pattern of her breathing as she slept again.

It hurt that she was being shut out. She knew how she'd felt even in the midst of the initial shock of learning that she was pregnant. That it was a miracle. Little beings were forming inside her belly. Her babies. She'd barely had time to get used to the idea either, but she already loved them enough to fight to the death to protect them.

But Kate had apparently been practising hiding her real feelings about Luke for a while now. Did she think that if she gave in to the grief she had to be experiencing now, it might not stop there? That she would confess she'd broken the rules of that stupid 'pact' they'd made at medical school to marry each other if they were both still single when they were thirty-five? That she *had* fallen in love and that Luke would call the whole thing off? She was pushing Luke away right now as well and that felt so, so wrong. They had found something very special between them and they should be fighting to protect it. This crushing blow should be bringing them closer together, not pushing them apart.

Georgia desperately wanted to help but she couldn't interfere, could she?

There was a barrier here that she had created herself because she hadn't wanted Kate to interfere with her own life by trying to influence her decisions. Because she hadn't ever shared the trauma of her own childhood. She hadn't told Kate that Matteo was the father of her babies. She hadn't even told her yet that she was carrying twins.

She certainly couldn't tell her that now, in the wake of her own loss that had to be devastating, even if Kate didn't want to admit it.

That barrier had just become a whole lot more solid.

The mess had just got a whole lot messier.

Something her mother had once quoted came back to her in the quiet hours of that night.

What a tangled web we weave, when first we practise to deceive...

Georgia couldn't even offer advice to her best friend to hang onto the connection she had found with Luke because they both knew how rare it was to find something like that. It would be a case of 'do what I say, not what I do', because she had found a connection herself that was just as rare and precious. With Matteo. And she was prepared to sacrifice that.

Not because she wanted to.

Because she *had* to.

She had to let her head win any battles with her heart because the lessons she had learned in life were so deeply engraved.

You couldn't trust love to last.

And some fathers could destroy your life.

There was a crazy moment, in those long hours where the silence was only broken by the sound of Kate's breathing, when it seemed that her heart could win the battle. Georgia seriously considered getting hold of Matteo's contact details and admitting the truth. The *whole* truth.

Her heart whispered encouragement. Maybe it was worth taking the risk. Maybe Matteo also knew how rare this kind of connection was and would be prepared to move heaven and earth to make it work.

But her head had plenty of ammunition left.

Are you crazy? You're expecting that kind of commitment on the strength of a couple of days and 'one' night together?

Maybe you imagined that the connection was mutual.

And do you really want to open that can of worms right now—when your very best friend is utterly miserable? Would you want to make her feel like she has to support you to chase the improbable dream of a happy-ever-after family when she's grieving for the loss of her own?

Kate's breath came out in a sigh that became a whimper of distress that was timed perfectly to underline just how wrong it would be to make this any worse than it had to be. Georgia smoothed a lock of blonde hair back from Kate's face and whispered reassuringly.

'It's okay… Everything's going to be okay.'

It had to be, that was all there was to it.

And, with that determination, another convincing victory got handed to her head. Georgia had chosen the path she needed to follow. Now she just needed to stick to it.

'Hey, man…' Matteo started speaking even before Luke's image came onto the screen of his laptop. The tone of the Skype call had interrupted the movie he was watching but it was a very welcome surprise. 'Where the hell have you been for the last few weeks?'

'It's been crazy.'

'You talking about your work or your love life?'

'Bit of both. Hey, before I get distracted, what are you doing on Friday?'

'Tomorrow or next week?' Matteo blinked. 'Not that it matters. I'm working on both Fridays. Why?'

'Do you reckon you could swap a shift? For next Friday? That gives you a whole week to sort it out.'

'I don't know.' Matteo peered at the screen but Luke didn't look as if he was in the midst of some personal crisis. He looked...very happy. 'It's never easy but I could try, I guess, if it was important enough. What's going on?'

'You remember what you said?'

'I say a lot of things.' Matteo grinned. 'What particular words of wisdom are you referring to?'

'That I can't get married unless you're my best man.' Luke was grinning back at him now.

'No *way*...' Matteo was stunned into silence for a long moment and then he shook his head. 'You are kidding, aren't you? You're getting married next week? What kind of notice is that?'

'I know, I'm sorry. We just got lucky in finding the perfect place. In an ancient chapel right in the middle of Edinburgh castle. You'd normally have to book a year or more in advance but we happened to ask on the same day an American couple had to cancel because they had some problem with their visas.'

Matteo was still trying to get his head around the news.

'You're getting *married*? Are you sure about this? I know we haven't talked for a while but this seems a bit sudden.'

'You haven't heard the half of it, mate. I told you things have been crazy—ever since Kate lost the baby...'

'Whoa...' Matteo sat up with a jerk that nearly sent his laptop flying. 'Kate was *pregnant*?'

'I know. It's a long story but it's okay now. We're going to try again. Made it harder on her that Georgia's pregnant as well but—'

'Cosa?' The knot in Matteo's gut made it feel like he'd just been kicked. 'Georgia's pregnant? *How* pregnant?' His heart skipped a beat as his mind flew in a totally crazy direction. She'd cheated on her boyfriend. Had she lied about it being a 'safe' time when he had taken her to bed himself?

'I don't know exactly...' Luke was blinking as if he was surprised at Matteo's interest. 'But I saw her a couple of days ago and I'd guess at least six months. She's got a pretty impressive bump.'

Matteo's brain was still processing information at the speed of light.

Six months? At *least*?

The competition had been about five months ago.

That would mean that Georgia had already been pregnant when she'd slept with him.

Had she *known*?

If she had, that made it far worse than simply cheating on someone.

'You can ask her yourself,' Luke said. 'She's going to be Kate's bridesmaid, of course.'

Matteo's jaw dropped. How could Luke actually be smiling at the prospect of him seeing Georgia again?

Because he didn't know, he reminded himself. Matteo had never told anyone what had happened that night.

Maybe Georgia had never told anyone either. If she had, surely it would have been her best friend and Kate was about to be married to *his* best friend and that meant they wouldn't have any secrets, didn't it?

He certainly wouldn't accept anything less than total honesty from someone he was about to promise to spend the rest of his life with.

But of course Georgia wouldn't have confessed. What if her boyfriend had found out?

He was probably more than that by now. He would have married her the moment he'd found out he was going to be a father, wouldn't he?

It was what he would do himself without a moment's hesitation. Family was sacred. Parents belonged with their children if it was at all possible and the bond had to be protected with everything you had.

Matteo didn't want to know if Georgia Bennett was already married.

He didn't want to see her again either. He'd believed he was completely over her now but this conversation had just flung open the mental door he'd thought he'd locked on that unfortunate blink of time in his life.

'So you'll come?' Luke's eyebrows rose hopefully. 'And be part of the best day of my life?'

This was his closest friend, asking him to do

something he'd vowed he *would* do. He needed to get over himself, didn't he?

And maybe it would be a good thing to see Georgia with her husband. With a baby on the way. Maybe then he could finally forget about her. For ever…

'I can't make any promises,' Matteo said slowly. 'But I'll see what I can do.'

CHAPTER SIX

IT WAS THE most perfect setting for a wedding.

The tiny stone chapel had an archway that Georgia and Kate would be making their entrance through any minute now. There was a soft glow of candlelight from within that warmed the surface of the ancient stones far more than the moonlight out here as the two women paused to wait for their signal.

The sound of bagpipes to accompany Kate on her walk down the aisle to meet the love of her life would also be perfect for this gorgeously Scottish wedding. Everything about this moment was making Georgia ridiculously happy— including the way that this soft, midnight-blue dress draped over the enormous bump of her belly and made her feel like a Madonna. Maybe not that beautiful but a perfect foil for how amazing Kate looked. Her dress had a fall of ivory silk that was brushing the cobblestones and an exquisitely bead-encrusted bodice with a sweet-heart neckline in the front and a deep V at the back. The bunch of pale peonies she was holding, with the silk bow that matched her dress, was simple and as elegant as everything else was turning out to be, but it was the glow of sheer joy on her face that really made her look more beautiful than Georgia had ever seen her look. She couldn't wait to start this new life with Luke, could she?

Suddenly Georgia couldn't wait either. Where was the piper who was due to start this ceremony?

'Oh, look…' There was a beat of excitement to add to her happiness now. 'I think that's him getting ready.' Her breath came out in a sigh. 'I do love a man in a kilt.'

She could hear the piper getting ready to play. Any moment now and those muffled squeaks as he filled the bag with air would burst into the full glory of her favourite musical instrument.

'Stand by…' she whispered loudly, her lips curving into a grin.

'No…' the call came from behind them. *'Wait…'*

Oh…*no…*

Georgia knew that voice. That *accent…*

Good grief… It felt like her bones were actually melting—possibly due to the weird explosion of every cell her in body, which was creating a tingling sensation that was so strong it was almost painful.

Both women turned in unison, so fast that Georgia's smile didn't have time to fade completely.

'Matteo…' Kate sounded overjoyed. 'You made it.'

'I didn't think I could. Not after the last delay with the fog.' Matteo must have run up all the steps to reach this part of the castle but he still looked immaculate in his black, beautifully tailored suit and a bow-tie nestled in the collar of a snowy, white shirt. With the soft moonlight, against the backdrop of this wonderful castle, he looked like an advertisement for some fashion house.

Just…impossibly gorgeous.

And it was having the same effect on her that it had had when she'd seen him for the very first time, at that competition briefing in Rakovi.

She needed to get a grip on this. Fast…

Matteo was still speaking. 'But I couldn't let my best friend get married without me.' He put his hand to his chest as he tried to catch his breath. He hadn't taken his eyes off this bride-to-be yet. Hadn't even looked at Georgia.

That hurt.

'You look…*bellissima*, Kate. Luke is a very lucky man.'

'He certainly is.' Georgia had to say something. To force Matteo to acknowledge her? Her heart was doing strange things—missing beats and then racing so fast it was scary.

No. *This* was scary.

Dangerous.

But…*thrilling* at the same time.

Oh, help… Why did she have to have this personality flaw that made danger so exciting? It was that addiction to an adrenaline rush that made her job such a part of who she was.

A part of why she had found such a compelling connection to this man. And being able to harness that adrenaline rush was part of what made her so good at her job but it was not a good thing as part of a personal relationship.

Not that she had a personal relationship with this man.

Not that she ever *could*.

'Hi, Matteo.' It was a test to see if she could actually say his name without giving away any of the shock that still clutched at her heart. It was a relief to find that she could.

She couldn't hold eye contact for more than a split second, however. Just that tiny brush and she could still feel it.

That connection.

Those impossibly powerful feelings that only this man had ever aroused.

Georgia flicked her gaze towards Kate, her message silent but probably desperate.

How could you not warn me?

How am I going to cope with this?

She *had* to cope, she had no choice. She managed to find a smile that said this was no big deal. To keep her tone just as casual. 'You didn't tell me Matteo was coming.'

'We really weren't sure that he could make it. Luke's going to be as surprised as you.'

Georgia couldn't help another glance at Matteo. Maybe it was just that first eye contact that would be so difficult.

But he wasn't looking at her face any longer. He was staring at her belly and, even in the moonlight that was already bleaching colour from skin, she could swear he had gone paler.

But…he didn't seem surprised. He looked angry more than shocked.

Had he *known* that she was pregnant? Had he put two and two together and was now preparing to make discover the truth and then make some kind of a claim?

Okay…this level of adrenaline was too much.

Any thrill was rapidly being buried under an avalanche of fear.

Matteo seemed to have lost his voice along with the colour. He opened his mouth and then closed it again. Then he cleared his throat.

'Hello, Georgia. You're looking…um…well?'

Fear was morphing into a determination that bordered on anger. How dared he turn up like this and threaten her?

Threaten her *babies*.

'I'm very well, thank you.'

She could see his chest move under the pristine white shirt. He was dragging in a deep breath.

'I'd better get inside.' Matteo was already moving away. 'Give me a minute to find my place, okay?'

Georgia watched him disappear through the archway just as the stirring first notes of the bagpipes filled the air around them.

Traditionally, the bagpipes were thought to have been a call to stir the passions of soldiers on the battlefield.

It certainly felt as if they were doing exactly that to Georgia.

She only had a few hours to fight to keep her secret safe somehow. She wasn't sure how she was going to do that but Georgia was quite sure she was going to win.

Because she had to.

She had lied to him before, even it if had only been the omission of correcting his assumption that she was cheating on someone. She could do it again. She was ready.

'Here we go,' Georgia said.

She pasted a bright smile onto her face. Not only did she have a private battle to fight, she was going to have to make sure it didn't lessen the joy of Kate's special day in any way.

'To have and to hold, from this day forward, till death us do part...'

The vows were traditional, but they were spoken by both Luke and Kate with a level of emotion that made them sound as if they had been written just for them. In the flicker of candlelight, within the ancient solidity of these historic walls, this ceremony was so beautiful it brought tears to Matteo's eyes.

He wanted this for himself, more than anything.

To promise himself to the woman he loved above any other. To know that he would never be alone. That he could begin the most important task he could ever achieve—to be a loving and devoted husband *and* father...

Even more than the desire to be standing where Luke was right now, holding the hands of the most beautiful bride ever, Matteo longed to be standing beside the woman who was shaped by the creation of his first child. Who had that superbly rounded belly and the glow of impending motherhood, exactly like Georgia did right now.

He'd never seen her look *so* beautiful...

Matteo stole a glance beyond Luke and Kate as they exchanged their rings and then found he couldn't take his gaze away from Georgia as she stood there, holding Kate's flowers, her eyes sparkling with what had to be unshed tears and a tiny tremor in her bottom lip that captured his heart and squeezed it like a vice.

He remembered exactly what it was like to feel that lip beneath his own. To feel the passion that was so much a part of this woman.

'With this ring, I thee wed... With my body I thee honour...'

The words about worldly goods became a blur of sound as Matteo grappled with the desire to be doing that to Georgia Bennett.

Honouring her.

Touching that magnificent belly with his hands. With his lips…

Dio mio… He needed to control himself better than this. For heaven's sake, the father of her child was most likely sitting in one of the wooden pews behind them. He would have to meet him very soon. Congratulate the man and tell him how lucky he was.

His glance finally jerked away from Georgia.

Who was he?

Perhaps that man in the second row who was sitting alone.

He looked a good ten years older than Georgia, with grey hair streaking a neatly trimmed beard and moustache. He was focussed on the ceremony and looked...content? As if he knew he was the luckiest man in the world?

Except, if he was Georgia's partner, he *wasn't* that lucky, was he? He was with a woman who had cheated on him.

Yes. This line of thought was helping a lot. His body—and his heart—might be telling him one thing but his head knew better. He just needed to remember what was most important in life and the one thing that meant Georgia could never be the perfect woman for him and he would be able to get through the next few hours without doing or saying anything that could lessen the joy of this occasion for Luke.

And then he could escape.

Champagne and canapés were to be served to guests in the Argyle Tower after the ceremony but there were some formal photographs to be taken before the bridal party could join the rest of the intimate group of the close friends chosen to share this occasion.

'Come with me,' the photographer ordered, after some shots outside the chapel. 'You can't not have the background of the whole castle behind you—it's a classic. We need to be just outside the main entrance.'

At least she wasn't alone with Matteo, Georgia reminded herself as she followed Kate and Luke towards the stone staircase. And it wouldn't take very long and then she could make sure she was always in the company of someone else. Dougal McGregor, her boss as the director of Edinburgh's Emergency Response Centre, was here by himself and would probably appreciate an introduction to many of the doctors from two of the major hospitals in their area.

In the meantime, however, nerves were kicking in. She had been able to lose herself in the actual ceremony as Kate and Luke had exchanged their vows to join their lives. Their love for each other was powerful enough to have taken her breath away and bring tears to her eyes.

And, if she was honest, a part of that emotional reaction was tinged with regret that she would never find this for herself—a loving partnership that could make her world feel so full of promise. So *safe*…

It wasn't that she hadn't searched for it. A psychoanalyst would probably say that she'd been searching her whole life because even her beloved mother hadn't been able to make her feel completely safe. How could she, when she'd never felt safe herself? Georgia knew that she had to take the blame for many of her own relationships foundering as well. The huge barrier of not being able to trust a man had been formed, brick by painful brick, as she'd grown up, and she'd never quite managed to climb over it. She'd tried. She'd believed she had been successful last time, with Rick, but that had come crashing down in spectacular fashion—as it inevitably did, time after time.

It's just not going to work, Georgie.
I feel like I have to try too hard all the time

and I don't even know what it is I'm supposed to be proving.

I'm sorry...but I've met someone else...

She needed love in her life, though. Who didn't? And Georgia knew she had always been destined to be a mother. That was the ultimately trustworthy love, wasn't it? Unconditional and fulfilling.

It would be enough.

She would protect her children with everything she had and, right now, there was a threat to them.

Their father.

It wasn't simply that he might know the truth and be about to make a claim either. Georgia was aware of a threat that came from within herself. This extraordinary pull that she felt towards Matteo was dangerous. Being this close to him, as the small group followed the photographer towards the staircase that led to the main entrance of the castle, was enough to have her whole body vibrating with awareness of him. Everything seemed more acute. She could feel every breath she was drawing in. The pale moonlight felt bright enough to be a spotlight.

And then, as they reached the first steps, Matteo was suddenly right beside her and his hand circled her elbow.

'Take care,' he said quietly. 'These steps are old and they could be slippery.'

Oh…dear Lord… The touch of his fingers against her bare skin took her straight back to that night. To those stolen hours of lovemaking that she could never forget.

Her head was telling her to pull her arm free. To smile politely and tell him that she was fine. Every other part of her was simply on strike. Any words refused to emerge. She could actually feel herself leaning into him, letting him support her balance, allowing her sense of touch to soak in the delicious heat that was making her skin tingle.

It was Matteo that broke the physical contact, dropping her elbow as if it was too hot to handle the moment they reached the bottom of the long staircase.

'We'll do the bride and groom first,' the photographer told them. 'Down here, so we've got you framed by the entrance archway and the braziers.'

Georgia and Matteo were left standing to one side.

Alone. Together.

'It's gorgeous, isn't it?' Georgia scanned the scene that would become the background of the image. There were spotlights on the turrets towering above them and the round sweep of the Half Moon Battery. Dramatic flames danced over the tall braziers that the bridal couple were positioned between. 'Perfect spot for a wedding, isn't it? Did you know that the chapel was built in the twelfth century?'

She could hear herself speaking too fast and would probably cringe when she remembered the artificially bright note in her voice.

'It's the oldest building in Edinburgh.' Her words slowed as she glanced sideways to catch the intent stare Matteo was giving her. 'Um… St Margaret's chapel, that is…'

'So, is he the man with the beard?' Matteo's tone was clipped.

'Sorry…what?'

'The man with the beard who was sitting in the second row.' He sounded impatient now. 'That's your husband?'

For a moment, Georgia was confused. If Matteo had known about her pregnancy, surely he would know that she didn't have a partner?

How much *did* he actually know?

Luke and Kate were kissing now. A tender moment that would make a fabulous photo to remind them of this occasion.

Georgia had to close her eyes in a long blink, however. Shame was pushing past confusion. Of course Matteo thought she had a partner. He believed she had been cheating on him when she'd gone to bed with *him*.

'That's Dougal McGregor,' she heard herself saying aloud. 'My boss.'

Matteo's breath came out in a silent whistle. 'The boss, huh? That's nice.'

Georgia's eyes snapped open. 'What's that supposed to mean?'

Matteo's gaze seemed to be fixed on Luke and Kate. They looked like they were sharing a joke now and Kate's head was tipped back as she laughed. Luke was grinning down as he held her in his arms. Maybe this would be the photo they kept on display, rather than the kiss, because they looked like the happiest two people on the planet.

Georgia was not happy. Matteo must have felt the anger in her glare because he turned his head. One eyebrow rose.

'You'll be well looked after,' he murmured. 'Even if you're not married.'

'Oh?' The single syllable was a warning but Matteo merely shrugged.

'He's the father of your baby, isn't he? Of course he will look after you.'

Anger got washed away in a small tsunami of relief.

He didn't know the truth.

This was it. A cloak of protection that she could wrap around herself and her babies.

Weirdly, there was disappointment to be found in finding safety so easily.

Man…she really was an adrenaline junkie, wasn't she? It was a personality trait that she really needed to squash, given that she was going to become a parent in the near future.

It wasn't going to be easy, though. The temptation to hint at the truth was irresistible.

'Dougal is not the father of my baby,' she told him, even as a part of her brain registered that Matteo had no idea that this was a twin pregnancy. 'And he's not the only person from my work who's here tonight so I'd appreciate it if you don't spread any unfounded rumours.'

Matteo was scowling at her, dark brows lowered over eyes that looked black in this light. 'But he *is* here? The father?'

Oh…the crazy part of her wanted to say 'yes' and flirt with danger again. But what if Matteo talked to everybody in the room over the canapés and champagne and worked out who that person could be by a process of elimination?

She could outright lie and say 'no' and make

safety even more assured but, despite what Matteo thought of her, it wasn't easy to tell a lie.

Her moment of hesitation provided an escape.

'Over here, you two,' the photographer called. 'We'll do the whole wedding party now, please.'

'What *is* this?'

Luke peered at the tiny sandwich Matteo had in his hand. 'I think that's the smoked salmon and horseradish crème fraîche. It's delicious.'

'Mmm…' Kate's head was leaning against her new husband's shoulder. 'We made some good choices, didn't we? Have you tried the Scottish beef and mustard mayonnaise ones? I've had three.'

'Oink-oink…' Luke dropped a kiss onto her hair.

Matteo put the sandwich into his mouth and let his gaze rake the room as he chewed it.

Where was she now?

It took only a split second to find Georgia, who was standing beside her boss. Had she been telling the truth when she'd denied that he was the father of her child? He could have sworn that when he'd asked whether that man was here, she'd been on the verge of confirming it. He could still feel an echo of the twist in his gut that was something bigger than jealousy. A betrayal almost. As if something that was rightfully his had been taken away.

It was crazy. He barely knew Georgia. They'd had only a matter of hours together.

So why was there a nagging conviction, he had never quite squashed, that she was the only woman in the world for him?

That he still loved her, despite the evidence that she had the worst fault a person could have as far as he was concerned.

Dishonesty...

He swallowed the mouthful of food that had suddenly become like cardboard.

'Who is it?' he surprised himself by asking aloud. 'The father of Georgia's baby?'

Kate's jaw dropped and Luke's eyebrows shot up.

'She won't say,' Luke offered into the slightly

awkward silence. Then he glanced at Kate, who bit her lip.

'I have my suspicions,' she confessed. 'I think it might be a paramedic from New Zealand that she…um…had a brief thing with.'

'New Zealand?' Matteo had to focus on something and this was easier than the idea that the father of Georgia's baby might not be in the picture any longer. 'Had' made it sound like ancient history. As if she had a space in her life that was glaringly empty. A space that *he* could fill…?

Could he do that? Not just get past the glaring fault of Georgia's lack of honesty but be able to be a father to someone else's child?

Sì…his heart whispered. Because it would mean you could spend the rest of your life with the woman you love…

No… His head shot back. Don't even think about it. Change the subject. A country on the other side of the globe was a *great* subject.

'Isn't that where you two are going on honeymoon?'

'More than that,' Luke said. 'I haven't had the

chance to tell you about it yet, but Katy and I are thinking of emigrating there. We've got some job interviews lined up for next week.'

'What?' Okay, this was an effective distraction. 'You're serious?' A pang of something like envy tightened his chest.

He was ready for something new.

An excitingly different challenge.

More people edged closer to congratulate Luke and Kate, which interrupted their conversation about how wonderful a country New Zealand was. Matteo drifted away—towards where Georgia was still standing with her boss. She must have seen him coming because she apparently spotted someone she was clearly keen to talk to and excused herself smoothly the moment he arrived by her side.

'It's Dougal, yes?'

The older man nodded. 'And you must be Matteo, the "paramedic extraordinaire" from Milan that Luke was telling me about.'

Matteo laughed. 'He trots that line out everywhere. I would take it with… How do you say it—a spoon of salt?'

Dougal grinned. 'A pinch. But he was very believable, I have to say. If you're ever in the market for a new job, come and have a chat. We have a position on our helicopter team coming up very soon that I'm keen to fill with someone extraordinary.'

'Oh?'

'We have a very international team. In the past, we've had guys from all over the world.' Dougal sighed. 'I guess the characteristics that make someone extraordinary include the desire for adventure and travel. Which is great, but it does mean that I have to go through this exercise of finding new people a lot more often than I'd like.'

Matteo nodded, but he wasn't feeling sympathy over Dougal's extra workload. His mind had stopped at the 'international' reference.

'Have you ever had someone from New Zealand working for you?'

Dougal blinked. 'As a matter of fact, we did. A while back now, though. Must be about six months since he left. It's *his* replacement that we're trying to find someone to fill right now. Why do you ask?'

'No reason.' Matteo didn't need to do the maths. It fitted. 'It just seems a popular part of the world at the moment.'

'Ah…because that's where Kate and Luke are planning to live?'

'Mmm.' Matteo's gaze was roving again and, of course, it settled on Georgia. Why was her boss here if it wasn't as her 'plus one'? Kate and Luke were both doctors and it seemed surprising that they would count the director of a rescue service as a close friend.

Dougal had followed the direction of his glance.

'You met Georgie, didn't you? At the rally in Rakovi?'

'Ah…yes.' Somehow, he managed to make it sound as if he had to try to remember. 'She was Kate's partner.'

Dougal nodded. 'She was the one who introduced me to Kate. We had her come to do some training sessions on station about dealing with paediatric trauma and we've been friends ever since. Have to say I'm delighted to share her happiness this evening.'

Matteo mirrored his nod. And, slowly, the smile. So there was a reason for Georgia's boss to be here tonight that meant he could let go of his suspicions.

And the probable father of her child was already back on the other side of the world, oblivious to what he'd left behind.

He took a sip from his drink as he relaxed.

'Tell me more,' he invited Dougal, 'about this job you have available…?'

CHAPTER SEVEN

IT WAS OVER.

The wedding guests followed the bridal couple down to the castle's entrance where a taxi was waiting to whisk them off to the luxury hotel they had chosen to celebrate their first night together as husband and wife.

Matteo was apparently staying in Luke's apartment for the night before he flew back to Italy tomorrow.

Georgia was going to drive back to the cottage that would feel very empty without Kate.

Her final hug with Kate was a fiercely tight one. The house wouldn't just feel empty for the three weeks that her best friend was on honeymoon.

Kate would never live with her again. Even if they weren't planning to emigrate to New Zealand in the near future, she would be living with Luke for the rest of her life, hopefully with the addition of children to complete their family.

Georgia was happy for them, she really was.

It was completely selfish to feel sad at the same time, wasn't it?

'I'm going to miss you,' she said.

'Same.' Kate had tears in her eyes as she finally let go.

Georgia found a smile. 'No, you won't. You'll be too busy living happily ever after.'

'That's not true and you know it.'

'What's not true?' Luke was beside Kate now. Holding her hand and about to urge her into their taxi.

'Kate doesn't think she's going to live happily ever after.'

'Oh?' Luke's glance at his new wife was so full of love it took Georgia's breath away. 'We'll see about that.'

Kate gave Georgia a long-suffering look. 'You'll keep. We'll talk soon, okay?'

Another quick hug and then the taxi pulled

away, the rattle of the traditional tin cans tied to the back of the car almost drowned out by the cheers of the guests.

And then there was a moment's silence before the murmur of people taking their leave.

'Where are you parked, Georgie?' Dougal McGregor asked. 'I'll walk you back to your car.'

'I can do that.' Matteo's voice came from behind them.

'I'm fine,' she said firmly. 'It's not far and there's plenty of people around. Thank you both, but I'm quite safe.'

Dougal smiled. 'See you at work tomorrow, then.'

'You will.' Georgia turned, intending to dismiss Matteo just as politely.

'Didn't Luke have a word with you?'

'Um…about what?'

'Giving me a lift to his apartment. He said it was on your way home.'

Georgia hadn't noticed the old leather satchel that Matteo must have had with him when he'd arrived. He adjusted the strap on his shoulder.

'No matter. I can get a taxi.'

They both looked at the empty street in front of them. Georgia closed her eyes for a moment. She had been too aware all evening of how the air around her changed when Matteo was present and her coping mechanism had been to keep as much space as possible between them. They were outside right now and the awareness was stronger than ever. Could she cope with being shut inside a small car with him?

She had to. She didn't want Kate finding out that she had let them down on their wedding night. Or maybe she didn't want to have to answer any questions about why it had been a big deal.

'It's not a problem,' she told Matteo. 'My car's this way.'

It wouldn't be a problem. It would take a matter of minutes, that was all.

She could cope with that breathless sensation of having this large man apparently using too much of the available oxygen in her vehicle. Of actually being aware of the warmth coming from his body that was only inches away from her own. Of the scent that was more alluring than any commercial aftershave.

Man…if some company could bottle the essence of Matteo Martini, they would make an absolute fortune…

What Georgia couldn't cope with, however, was that Matteo didn't get out of the car when she pulled up at Luke's address. He just sat there, staring out of the windscreen until the silence became unbearable.

She flinched at the low rumble of his voice when Matteo broke the silence.

'I need you to tell me something.'

Oh, *no*… Georgia felt as if any safety barriers around her had just evaporated. She was standing on the edge of a cliff and the slightest wrong move would be catastrophic.

Matteo didn't wait for her to respond. He still wasn't even looking at her.

'Did you know,' he asked quietly, 'that you were already pregnant that night? Is that why you said it was safe?'

Here it was. An opportunity to ensure that Matteo would never know the truth. That she would be safe for ever from having the father of her children try to interfere with her life in any way.

All she had to do was say 'yes'.

But she couldn't do it.

If she said 'yes' she would be tarnishing the memory of the most perfect night of her life. Turning it into something that Matteo would dismiss as being even worse than cheating on someone.

Her breath came out in a sigh of surrender.

'No. I didn't know.'

'But you were.' She could actually hear Matteo's painful swallow. 'Already pregnant when we were together.'

A flash of memory engulfed Georgia. She was in his arms again. He was filling her and her name was a groan of ecstasy as Matteo joined her in paradise.

Any science behind the timing of the conception was irrelevant. As far as Georgia was concerned, *that* was the moment she had become pregnant.

'Yes,' she whispered.

She never cried. But she had to blink hard right now.

'And you're happy about it?'

Good grief… It sounded as if Matteo was on the verge of tears as well.

It was Georgia's turn to swallow hard. 'Yes. I've wanted a baby for a long time.'

'But you're not with the father.'

'No.'

'Have you got family that will help you?'

'No.'

Another long silence fell. It felt different this time. Not threatening at all. Almost sad, in fact.

How could anyone be facing a future like Georgia's when they didn't have the support of a loving family?

Even trying to imagine it was breaking Matteo's heart.

It was brave and he admired that courage very

much but it wasn't the way things should be. Especially for Georgia. She needed to be adored.

The way *he* could adore her…

His mother and sisters would love her, too. And their children would be part of a tribe of cousins when they gathered to celebrate family occasions like birthdays or Christmas. Nobody would need to know that their first child wasn't his own because he would love it as if it were.

Because it would be part of Georgia and he'd never quite managed to stop loving her.

He took hold of Georgia's hand and broke the silence.

'I will help you,' he said. 'I could be a father to your baby, Georgia.'

She looked totally shocked. Her mouth started to open but no words came out. She was clearly too stunned to say anything. Or even move to pull her hand away when Matteo raised it to his lips and pressed a kiss to her knuckles.

Dio mio, but his heart was winning this time. Hanging onto that image of the future when his own family was a part of a joyous, Martini gathering. The only branch of the family tree that could carry on the name, in fact.

He would be so proud to do that.

And he wanted Georgia as his partner.

He hadn't intended to say his next words but somehow he had to convey just how genuine his offer to help was. How deeply he was prepared to commit to being with both Georgia and her unborn child.

'Marry me,' he said.

CHAPTER EIGHT

So…

Here he was…

Doing the craziest thing he'd ever done in his life.

Matteo Martini paused as he reached the top of the spiral staircase that led from the enormous helicopter hangar to the offices and staff quarters above.

The bright red overalls of his new uniform felt a little stiff and he rubbed the side of his neck where the coarse material was irritating his skin. A glance through the wall of glass beside him made him pause for a moment.

Edinburgh's Emergency Response Centre was an impressive set-up. This hangar and the tarmac where the helicopters were parked were side by side with the land-based arm of the ambulance service. He could see the huge building that housed the control centre and quarters for the dozens of paramedics who worked here. There was an astonishing number of ambulances lined up outside the building and a row of the SUVs that were painted in the same colours, with beacons on the top. They had similar vehicles in Milan, where experienced paramedics could be sent as a first response or backup to ambulances.

He could see one of these cars heading out as the automatic gates slid open. As soon as it outside the gates, he could see that the driver activated the beacons and he could hear the faint wail of a siren.

Matteo took a very deep breath.

It could be Georgia. Luke had told him that she was currently employed in one of those cars.

He assumed that she didn't know that he had taken this job on the helicopter team. Why would she? The land and air services might work closely together but these bases were separate entities. It might, in fact, prove difficult to see much of Georgia.

Especially given that she wouldn't want to be seeing *him*.

Okay. Perhaps taking this new job in a strange city wasn't the craziest thing he'd ever done.

That prize had to go to proposing marriage to a woman he'd only spent one night with. A woman who'd made it very clear that night, a couple of weeks ago, that she didn't need a man to help her.

Didn't *want* one.

And yet here he was. Making himself available. Putting himself on the line in a way that would have been incomprehensible for any other woman he'd ever met.

Why?

Because he hadn't been able to talk himself out of it, that's why. It just felt…right. He'd convinced himself that, if nothing else, this could be a good career move. He could get experience in things that were hard to come by in a huge city like Milan. Mountain rescues perhaps. Or working in difficult conditions, like deep snow. It would be an adventure.

The fact that it was the only first step he could

think of on a journey that could lead to Georgia changing her mind about him was irrelevant.

It had to be. Matteo started moving again. Dougal had given him a comprehensive tour of this facility yesterday and he would be waiting to introduce him to the new team of his paramedic partner and their pilot. His first shift was about to begin.

The new pager clipped to his belt could sound at any moment.

Matteo felt his heart rate kick up a notch. This was one of the things he loved about this job. You never knew when something was going to happen. Or what challenges it could present.

He was ready.

For anything.

The crescendo beat of an approaching helicopter had never been so welcome.

Georgia known that something was wrong as soon as she'd arrived on scene and approached the huddle of people at the bottom of the hill in this mountain biking park on the outskirts of Edinburgh.

A ground-based ambulance crew was already here and, when she saw the look of relief on the young paramedics' faces when they noticed her arrival, it was obvious that this situation was well out of any comfort zone.

At first glance, she couldn't understand what was disturbing them so much. Automatically assessing the scene for safety and any clues about what kind of injury she might need to treat, Georgia had already noticed a bicycle with a very bent wheel amongst the undergrowth and the young boy who was lying on his side, apparently unconscious. A group of other pre-teen children were grouped well away, clutching the handlebars of their bikes, and there were adults with them who were wearing blue polo shirts with a logo that had a bike in mid-air as it cleared an obstacle. Was this a school trip to an adventure park perhaps?

More adults in the blue shirts and a couple in civvies were close to the injured boy and one of the paramedics was taking a blood pressure. That suggested that the child was still alive but the expressions on the faces she could see were telling a different story.

And the silence was unnerving.

There was no time to waste on friendly introductions to a junior crew she didn't recognise. Georgia slipped her arms from the backpack with all her gear and dropped to a crouch, realising belatedly that the size of her belly made this impractical so she ended up on her knees beside her patient.

'Fill me in,' she directed quietly, her fingers already on the boy's neck, feeling for a pulse.

'This is Toby,' one of the paramedics told her. She was holding the boy's shoulders. Preventing him from being moved? 'He's eleven years old. He's come off his bike at speed, going downhill.'

A head injury? Georgia glanced at the helmet the boy was still wearing. She couldn't see any evidence of damage.

The pulse she could feel beneath her fingers

was light and rapid. A little uneven, which was a concern.

Was he bleeding out from a severed artery?

Another searching glance didn't show her any signs of blood loss and surely even the most junior crew would have external bleeding well under control by now.

'He hit this tree. And...'

The tiny hesitation in the paramedic's voice came at the same instant that Georgia saw what the problem was.

It had looked as if the small branch that had snapped from the tree was just a part of the organic debris of this crash scene.

But only one end of the branch was visible.

The other end was hidden beneath a fold in the material of this young boy's shirt. Very gently, Georgia moved the material and her heart sank.

Just how far had this stick penetrated? Were the irregular beats she had noticed due to its proximity to Toby's heart?

This was beyond serious. It was critical.

The people all looking to her for guidance were

probably reassured by how calmly she spoke. It was a skill honed over a long career of facing difficult situations. She might be on the verge of panicking but nobody would ever guess.

'Can you get on the radio to Comms, please,' she said to the first paramedic. 'Request urgent helicopter backup and then organise a place for it to land.' She turned to the second crew member. 'I need padding so that we can stabilise this branch. Then I'll need my IV roll out of my pack and I want you to get some ECG electrodes in place. Very carefully.' She looked up at the bystanders. 'Can I get someone to come and hold Toby's shoulders, please? And someone else to keep a hand on his legs? We have to make sure we don't move him yet, even an inch.'

By the time she heard the approach of the helicopter, Toby had IV fluids running, oxygen on, and a monitor that was recording his heart rhythm and blood pressure. Georgia had her hands on the doughnut-shaped padding that was around the base of the stick. She didn't know how close it was to this boy's heart but she could feel the movement of its beating and knew that even a small movement of the impaled object could prove fatal.

She was so focussed on what she was doing, she didn't even look up until a flash of red filled her peripheral vision. The legs of one of the critical care paramedics from the helicopter crew. Her glance flicked up swiftly and—despite that skill of keeping a personal reaction hidden in the face of a difficult situation—it was a miracle that her hands remained rock steady when she saw the face beneath the helmet.

Matteo?

The flicker on his face told her that her shocked thought must have escaped in an audible gasp but he wasn't about to waste a split second on any explanation.

'Vital signs?'

'Blood pressure and oxygen saturation have dropped in the last five minutes and the blood pressure's widened. Respiratory rate increasing. He's in sinus rhythm but I'm worried about an increasing number of ectopic beats. I'm querying a cardiac tamponade?'

Matteo was unhooking a stethoscope from around his neck.

'I'm going to check his breathing and heart sounds. I'll work around you. Don't move.'

Of course she wasn't going to move. Even if the 'fight or flight' part of Georgia's brain had activated itself and was urging her to flee.

To get away from Matteo.

A man who had offered to marry her and help raise what he believed to be another man's child.

She'd known that Italian men had the reputation of being passionate and impulsive but that had been the craziest thing she'd ever heard. That the offer had actually been as alluring as it was appalling was what had made it so dangerous. Fear had prompted the rush of words she had finally found to respond to him. To tell him that she didn't want him, or *any* man, in her life. He'd finally got out of her car and left—as silently as he had that night after he'd left her bed. And that, she had been quite confident, was the end of it all.

But here he was.

And a traitorous part of her brain was registering something like…happiness?

No. It was probably simply relief that people even more qualified than she was were here to help manage this critical situation where a small boy's life was at stake.

'Thank goodness you're here.' A male bystander who might be Toby's teacher was watching Matteo as he moved the disc of the stethoscope over the boy's chest and he seemed to share Georgia's relief. 'You'll know what to do.'

A flick of a glance from Matteo told Georgia that she'd been doing exactly the right thing to keep Toby safe until she had the backup she needed.

'Can you pull it out?' One of the female bystanders, perhaps a parent helper, sounded terrified. 'It's going to kill him, isn't it?'

'Pulling it out would be the worst thing to do,'

Georgia responded quietly. 'It might even be saving his life at the moment.'

'What?' The man was incredulous now. 'You've got to be kidding me.'

Matteo glanced up as he reached to open his pack. 'If a foreign object has penetrated something important, like a major blood vessel, it can be the pressure of the object that's stopping uncontrollable bleeding.' He turned back to meet Georgia's gaze.

'I need you to keep the stick really still while I do as best as I can with an ultrasound. I need to know if this is a cardiac tamponade or a haemothorax. We'll need to cope with either of those scenarios before we can move him.'

'We'll also need to shorten this before we can get him in the chopper.' Matteo's crew partner was examining the length of the branch. 'I'll check that we've got a saw on board.'

Matteo's eased the small transducer of the portable ultrasound amongst the shreds of fabric where Georgia had already cut Toby's clothing clear. He was very gentle as he edged around the gauze padding that Georgia was holding firmly in place around the entry point of the stick. His hands brushed hers and, at one point, the back of his hand pressed directly onto hers as he took a closer look at the image on the screen.

'Look at that. You can see that the ventricle wall is functioning. There's no blood loss with the contractions that's going into the pericardium.'

Georgia skirted the awareness of the touch of his skin against her own. Except that it was actually helping her own concentration on this emergency. Making her feel as if she wasn't alone in trying to save this young life. That, together, the chance of success had somehow more than doubled.

'So it's a haemothorax?'

'Haemopneumothorax, probably. Same effect. I can see that air movement has decreased on this side even in the time it took to do the ultrasound.'

'Are you going to do a needle decompression?'

'Yes. I'd rather put in a drain but getting him

to Theatre is the priority. It's only ten minutes' flying time and a needle decompression should be enough.'

For the next few minutes, Georgia watched both members of the helicopter crew working but she could do nothing to help except keep her position and keep this stick as stable as possible, especially when Matteo's partner, Shane, was carefully sawing the branch to leave a length that would be manageable as they transported him.

Matteo was working remarkably swiftly. As soon as he noted that Toby was not unconscious enough to be feeling no pain from the vibration of the stick as it was carefully sawn through, he drew up drugs and administered them into the IV line Georgia had already established. When the needle inserted between the small ribs failed to release enough pressure to improve breathing, he and Shame worked as a team to perform the surgical procedure to insert a proper drain and remove some of the blood that was preventing a lung from functioning.

It was impressive.

And then they were ready for the delicate task of moving their young patient to the stretcher and into the helicopter.

'Can you come with us?' Matteo asked Georgia. 'I know we can trust you to keep that stick stable.'

She still hadn't let go of the padding around this object and she didn't want to until she knew that Toby was safe.

'We can get your vehicle back to base,' one of the original paramedics on scene said.

Georgia nodded. But the next few seconds were anxious ones. She had to get up off her knees as they lifted the stretcher without moving her hands and changing the pressure that was keeping the stick steady. Normally that wouldn't have been a problem but she had a huge belly that was affecting her balance now and couldn't know whether it was going to be a problem.

Matteo's sharp glance as she began to move told her that he was thinking along the same lines. He jerked his head at one of the ambulance crew to take his place at the head of the stretcher to lift it and he stepped behind Georgia, putting his hands under her arms to grip her body and help her to her feet.

The strength in those hands and arms was astonishing.

It was entirely inappropriate to even notice that they were in contact with more than her ribs but her body overrode her focus for just a heartbeat. Later—probably in the middle of the night—it would remind her that her breasts remembered that fleeting touch. And that would remind her of so much more...

It was just as well that there were too many other things to focus on right now. It was Georgia's job to keep the foreign object stable as the others worked around her. To keep her gaze on the monitor at all times and warn of any changes to vital signs like heart rhythm, oxygen saturation and blood pressure.

And part of her was savouring every moment of this adrenaline-filled mission. Her peripheral vision showed the mountain park scene fall away beneath them as the helicopter took off, and Georgia knew this might be the last challenge like this that she would have for a very long time. She knew her baby bump could have interfered with her doing her job if Matteo and Shane hadn't been there.

She'd held onto her front-line job for as long as she could but it really was time to step down and spend the next few months in an environment that was safer for everybody. The patients, herself and her babies.

And, maybe, that would also keep her well away from Matteo's orbit. That was something else that would be haunting her later tonight when she had the head space to revisit the shock of his reappearance in her life.

Georgia had no idea how she was going to cope with it.

Or even if she could.

Well…that had been a memorable first day on a new job.

He'd been right that this position was going

to give him new experiences and enhance his skills.

Matteo paced the floor in Luke's small apartment in central Edinburgh, heading for the fridge in the hope of finding a cold beer.

That job this morning, with the young boy impaled by the branch, had been exciting. Challenging. That they'd got him to the hospital and into Theatre with no major deterioration in his condition had been a triumph. He would contact the intensive care unit tomorrow and ask for an update. Have a chat with the specialist in charge of his case, hopefully.

Because having an update to share would give him an excuse to make contact with Georgia?

No. That wasn't his motivation. He needed to know how his patient was doing. Whether he'd done everything he should have done on scene.

The fact that he would have a reason to get in touch with Georgia to pass on the information was simply a bonus.

But Matteo sighed as he twisted the top off the small bottle.

He was facing a bigger battle than he'd expected.

That look of shock on her face in the instant when she'd recognised him today.

Horror, almost… Or perhaps even *fear*?

What was that about?

How could you find a connection with someone that was *this* powerful and then not want to explore it further?

How could you make love with someone like that and not be desperate to try it again? To see if it really was the most extraordinary experience in your life?

Unless she hadn't felt the same way.

No. Matteo didn't believe that. The lines of physical communication had been the clearest he'd ever experienced. It hadn't made any difference that they came from different countries. They had been speaking exactly the same language that night.

Okay… Maybe he'd scared her by that impulsive offer of marriage. He could understand that. He'd been carried away in the moment. If she'd said 'yes', he would have put his heart and soul into making it work, but he was quite prepared to take this more slowly and win her heart.

But he'd never come across a barrier quite like this.

He had been left with the impression that Georgia *was* actually afraid of him and that was deeply disturbing.

Had it been his anger when he'd thought she was cheating on someone else by being with him that night? It wasn't as if he'd threatened her in any way. He hadn't even raised his voice. He'd simply walked away and then ignored her from that point on.

Maybe the anger had been enough.

Had Georgia been abused at some point in her life by an angry man? A boyfriend, perhaps. Or... her father?

The thought made him sick.

Whatever the reason, however, he could feel proud of the courage Georgia was showing, being faced with a situation she had made very clear was something she didn't want.

She had done her job, working so closely with

him, with professionalism and skill. After that initial shock, there hadn't been any hint that she was distracted by anything personal. Even when he'd held her body to help her to her feet. She hadn't flinched. He would have felt the slightest tremor beneath his hands and, if anything, she'd let him take more weight than strictly necessary.

As if she'd welcomed his assistance. Trusted him to deliver it.

But the fact that the assistance had been welcome bothered him as well. Why was she still working on the front line like this when she was at such an advanced stage of her pregnancy? Surely there was a cut-off point when it wasn't allowed to happen?

She needed protection, even if she didn't think she did. Matteo took a long swallow of his beer. He might have a chat to Dougal tomorrow and just ask. Carefully. He didn't want to antagonise Georgia. She'd been clearly taken aback by finding out that her friend hadn't warned her he was arriving.

It had been a rather disappointing conversation

all round, actually, when they'd finally left Toby in the hands of the operating theatre's team.

'Why Scotland? Why *here*?' Georgia had demanded, keeping her gaze on the long corridor ahead of them.

'Why not? I was ready for a new adventure and I happened to be offered a job when I was here for the wedding.'

'And Luke knew you were coming?'

'Of course. He offered me his apartment to live in.'

'But they're coming back. Next week. You're planning to live with a newly wed couple?'

'No. But they'll only be here for a brief time. To pack everything up and go to their new life in New Zealand. Kate said it wouldn't be a problem. She knew a place I could use.'

'So Kate knew, too?' Georgia had looked wounded. 'She didn't tell *me*.'

'I asked them not to. I wanted it to be a surprise.'

'Oh…' She made a hollow sound that wasn't quite laughter. 'I'm surprised…'

'Kate thought it was a good idea.'

'What? You coming to work in Edinburgh?'

'That I would be here for you, *cara*. That you would have a friend.' Yes, he had seen a flash of alarm in her eyes. He couldn't risk pushing her. 'If you need one, that is.'

'We're not going to be friends, Matteo.'

'Why not?'

'Because…' She was avoiding his gaze. 'Just because…'

He didn't sigh audibly. But if he was prepared to try getting past the fact that she'd lied to him, surely Georgia could get past whatever it was that was making her keep him at arm's length? No, it was more than arm's length. She would prefer the length of a whole country.

'We *could* be.' He'd given her his most persuasive smile when they'd parted company at the elevators. He was heading for the helipad on the roof and Georgia was going to catch a ride back to base with the next available ambulance crew. 'It might even be nice.'

* * *

A few days later, Georgia was at the airport late in the evening to collect Kate and Luke as they returned from their honeymoon. The anticipation of how good it was going to be to see her best friend for the first time in weeks was lifting her spirits for the first time in what seemed ages.

The last few days had been tough.

Her heart wanted to fill her thoughts with memories of Matteo Martini but her head drowned them with worry about the implications of him having anything to do with her life. Of him somehow finding out the truth.

Of *wanting* him to know the truth?

Yes. That was part of it. It wasn't just that her body and heart kept reminding her of the connection she felt with Matteo. This was making her feel guilty.

Telling her that she'd done something very wrong. No. That she was *still* doing something very wrong and it didn't sit well at all. It had been far easier to bury the guilt when the father of her children had been in another country and the chance of seeing him again had been remote.

Her heart also wanted to grieve a little for stepping away from her work on the road and her head was determined to find something good about being given a desk job. The research task of a retrograde data collection to identify the most effective airway adjunct to use in a cardiac arrest could potentially change protocols. It should be exciting. It was certainly a lot better than doing some kind of massive stocktake, except that if her hands had been busy at the same time, perhaps her brain wouldn't stray quite so often.

Back to the unexpected bombshell in her life. At least she had anticipated the change of lowering her workload.

She had never expected Matteo to reappear in her life.

And she hadn't expected to see him now but that tall back beneath the electronic flight arrivals board was unmistakeable.

'For God's sake, Matteo,' she snapped, when she was right behind him, a little gratified that it made him jump. 'What are *you* doing here? Kate arranged for me to collect them before they even left.'

'And Luke texted me before they took off from Dubai.' A dark eyebrow rose. 'Perhaps they have a great deal of luggage?'

Georgia glanced at the board. The plane had landed on time so they should be coming through Customs any minute now.

'Or perhaps you missed a call about a change of arrangements,' Matteo suggested mildly. 'You don't seem to like answering your telephone.'

Georgia could feel a blush of colour creeping into her cheeks. She *had* deliberately ignored the call from Matteo the day after they'd worked together. She had actually deleted the voicemail before listening to it, because she hadn't wanted to listen to his voice. That sexy, deep rumble. That accent...

It was inexcusably rude, given that Matteo was Luke's best friend. And Luke was now *her* best friend's husband. It wasn't just that connection either. Matteo was now part of her own branch of the emergency services and it was a close-knit community.

One way and another, she was going to have to spend time with Matteo, at least in the near future.

She really needed to get a grip on how she was going to manage that.

An apology for her rudeness might be a good first step?

'Sorry,' she mumbled. 'I've been really busy. What was it that you wanted to talk about?'

'Just that case we shared on my first day. Toby. You remember him?'

'Of course. An impalement injury like that is a once-in-a-lifetime type of job.' Curiosity got the better of her. 'Did you follow up on him? How *is* he?'

'Probably ready to go home. He was one very lucky little boy. That stick had actually penetrated his left ventricle but because it wasn't removed until he was in Theatre, the bleeding was easily controlled and the damage repaired. Antibiotic treatment prevented an infection and he only needed a short time in Intensive Care for monitoring after the surgery.'

'Oh…that's fantastic news.' Georgia's smile was genuine. 'What a great job to have done on your first day. You handled it brilliantly.'

'*We* handled it brilliantly,' Matteo corrected.

The corner of his mouth tilted in a crooked grin and, for a moment, it was like the first time she'd ever spoken to him. When she was completely captured. Flustered enough, even, to say something pretty stupid.

'Hey… Good to see you two getting along so well.'

'*Luke*…' Georgia and Matteo both spoke at the same time as they turned away from each other.

'And *Katy*,' Georgia added, throwing her arms around her friend with relief, both to see her again but also to have her attention so thoroughly diverted from Matteo. 'Oh…it's *so* good to see you.'

'We're going to have lots of time to catch up in the next couple of weeks while I work out my notice. I can't wait to tell you about New Zealand. And show you photos. You won't believe how beautiful it is. You should think about emigrating, too, Georgie.'

Matteo was walking ahead of them beside Luke, who was pushing the luggage trolley.

'Maybe I will,' Georgia murmured. 'Hey, do you want to go home in my car? Matteo could take Luke, seeing as we've doubled up on chauffeurs.'

Kate's eyes widened with something that looked a lot like guilt.

'What?' Georgia demanded. 'What's going on?'

'Um… I told Matteo I'd found a place for him to stay while we were back in town. I was hoping you'd give him a lift.'

It was something to do with that hopeful little smile on Kate's face that planted the seeds of a suspicion that rapidly grew into disbelief.

'You *didn't*…'

'It seemed logical. A place to stay and he can use my car until I sell it. And you two are getting on better now, aren't you? You might even like him, Georgie, if you gave him a chance. Luke's told me all about Matt and he's a *great* guy…'

Her friend was matchmaking.

Worse than that, this was like an intervention. Kate and Luke had come up with a plan that would force their best friends to spend a whole lot of time together.

To *live* together…

'No.' Georgia was struggling to find words. 'You can't do this, Kate. Matteo wouldn't want it any more than I do.'

Kate ducked her head. 'Sorry…' She offered a tentative smile. 'It doesn't have to be for the whole time but it's a bit late to find something else tonight and a bit rude to stick him in some hotel. He could sleep on our sofa, I guess.'

Luke was putting the bags into the boot of his car now. Matteo was pulling a bag from the back seat. He smiled at Georgia, eyebrows lifted.

The smile was an echo of the one they had shared so recently when they'd been talking about Toby. When, for a heartbeat, she'd forgotten the barrier between them.

'You don't mind, do you? Dropping me at my new place?'

So he didn't know he'd been offered Kate's old room in the cottage.

How would he react when he found out?

Oh…this was playing with fire if anything was.

And some wicked part of Georgia wanted to poke the embers. Like the first time she'd spoken to him, unexpected words that she could well regret later simply slid past her lips.

'No problem. It's not out of my way at all…'

CHAPTER NINE

'I'M SORRY, GEORGIA. I had *no* idea.'

Matteo had looked surprised when Georgia opened the door of the cottage with her own keys. And then he'd looked stricken as the penny had dropped.

'I know.' She shrugged. 'I think Kate and Luke have got this idea that we could…that we might…'

Matteo pushed his fingers through his hair. 'Take me back to town. I can find a hotel.'

The fact that it was Matteo who didn't want to be here perversely made Georgia more inclined to let him stay.

It was a battle between her head and her heart that was being played out in real life instead of in her imagination. And right now her heart was winning.

'It's okay. As Kate said, it's logical. You need a place to stay for a little while. There's an empty room here. For tonight anyway.'

'I would never force myself on you like this. You know that, don't you?'

Oddly, Kate *did* know that. Instinctively, she knew that this man's moral code would prevent him from ever hurting anyone—especially a woman—with no consideration taken for any personal injury that could be the result.

This situation should have been making her more afraid than ever.

But, weirdly, it was making her feel safer.

This was her turf and she was in control. And it *was* an intervention in a way that Kate knew nothing about.

Georgia didn't want to live with unresolved guilt for the rest of her life. Being under the same roof as Matteo was going to force her to find the solution, wasn't it?

Not that she had any idea what that solution might be, mind you.

Emigrating to New Zealand was starting to seem like less of a crazy idea...

By the time Georgia got up the next morning, Matteo was already gone. There wasn't even a dirty cup in the sink to suggest that he'd been in the kitchen but she could sense that he had been.

It felt different...

As if the emptiness of her house over the last few weeks had been smudged around the edges.

How had he managed to be so tidy? And so quiet? Had Matteo actually slipped out of the house at some point during the night and gone off to find a hotel?

The notion should have been a relief but it was curiously alarming at the same time. So much so that Georgia climbed the stairs again, which was getting to be quite an effort, in order to peep around the partially open door of Kate's old room.

Matteo's leather satchel lay on floor in front of the wooden chair in the corner of the room. The clothes he'd been wearing last night were carelessly draped over the back of the chair.

Georgia's breath came out in a sigh that felt like relief.

He was coming back, then…

Her gaze drifted sideways to the bed. The patchwork quilt had been pulled up but it wasn't as smooth as Kate would have left it. She could almost see the indent of where Matteo's body had been.

Her breath got stuck. Maybe that was why she was feeling a bit weird. Dizzy even…

There was definitely an edge of confusion.

Her hours of work were far more relaxed now, so Georgia had time to sit in the sun with her cup of tea and toast. Time to explore what it was that was nagging at the back of her mind and causing her confusion.

She missed Kate. This was the best thing about having a bestie. You got to think aloud and the supportive audience could help pinpoint not only what the real issue was but what you wanted to do about it.

But she couldn't bat this around with Kate. She was on her own.

And it wasn't that hard to mentally tiptoe closer to what she was afraid to look at so closely.

All it took was to allow an image of Matteo Martini to fill her mind. Those dark eyes that could see too much. That layer of genuine interest and concern in combination with a smile that was undeniably sinful.

He just oozed charm, didn't he?

But he also made her feel safe.

I would never force myself on you like this. You know that, don't you?

Of course he wouldn't. He had a moral code that was so iron clad, he would never dream of lying. Or cheating on someone. He would simply walk away from someone who didn't share those values.

But he'd come back…

Because of her? Because the significance of what they'd found with each other was enough to be making him reconsider those iron-clad rules?

Because he really did want to be her *friend*?

No. He wanted to be more than that. He'd offered to marry her, for heaven's sake. To be a father to her child.

And now he was here but he'd taken a huge step back. He was leaving it up to her to choose whether she closed the respectful gap he was keeping.

No wonder she was confused.

Matteo was nothing like any man she had ever known.

Certainly *nothing* like her father...

And there it was. The real issue.

What if her father had used charm instead of violence? If he'd simply been there in her life and let her make a choice of whether she wanted him closer or not? If a genuine concern for her welfare and happiness had been there in his eyes and he'd had a smile that suggested she was the only person in the world who mattered at that moment?

Life would have been very different, wouldn't it?

She could have lived her early life without the fear of that pain—both emotional and physical.

She could have been like the kids she'd envied

so much. The ones who'd had a daddy at home to tease them sometimes but protect them always.

Oh, boy…this was huge. Georgia tried to stop the thought that was coming at her as relentlessly as a tsunami but she couldn't.

Did she *really* want her children to grow up without a father?

It was almost as if she had Kate sitting here with her. Understanding at least part of her new dilemma. Asking her what she wanted to do about it.

Suggesting that the only the thing to do might be to tell Matteo the truth.

The shock of allowing that possibility any head room at all was enough to push Georgia to her feet.

She needed to get to work. To work so hard, in fact, that she could close the lid of this 'too hard' basket very firmly indeed.

'Oh, my God…what is that smell?'

'Lasagne. A secret recipe that's been handed down in my family for generations.'

'You can *cook*?'

'Anyone who bears the Martini name has to know how to make the perfect lasagne. Just ask any one of my sisters.'

'Oh…' Georgia let the bag full of the papers she had brought home slip from her hand.

She was late. Coming home to a house that had its lights twinkling in the darkness had been a lift all by itself. Entering a kitchen that was redolent with the most delicious smell she had ever encountered was actually overwhelming enough to make her feel unsteady on her feet.

Maybe that was because her feet were so swollen today. Or that she'd been pushing herself so hard at work for the last week or more that she was exhausted. It had worked, though. Any issues that were bothering her hadn't been allowed any significant head space and Matteo had made it easier out of work hours, too, with the way he had been using her home as little more than a hotel, always gone so early and often back so late their paths had barely crossed.

Which made this scenario even more blind-siding.

'You've been working too hard,' Matteo told her. 'And I've been rude. I've hardly been here. I had a night out with the guys from work. With Luke. At the gym. Anyway… This is my way of saying thank you. Please…sit down. I thought it would be more comfortable for you on the couch. Can I get you something to drink?'

There was bottle of red wine open on the coffee table in the small sitting room, between a basket of freshly sliced baguette and a bowl of what looked like a very crispy green salad.

The wine was tempting but Georgia's hand went automatically to her belly, where it was rewarded with the bump of a kick from a tiny foot.

'A water would be great.'

'Sparkling or still?'

'Oh…sparkling, please. I could pretend it's champagne.'

'Which is exactly why I bought some.' Matteo's smile curled more widely. 'I hadn't forgotten your preference.'

He had brought a chilled bottle of champagne to the table at the end of the competition, hadn't he? For her. The first move in that dance that had led them to its memorably intimate conclusion.

Georgia sank onto the couch. The wave of emotion threatened to drown her but she was too tired to fight.

Maybe she could just float for a while, she decided, easing off shoes that had become far too tight.

Every mouthful of this unexpected dinner was delicious, possibly because of far more than the actual taste of the food. What was astonishingly powerful was this feeling of being cared for.

Of feeling…safe…

Oh, man… Georgia took a large gulp of her water. She hadn't been this close to crying since she'd first found out she was pregnant. Or when she'd been standing there in that ancient chapel, listening to Luke and Kate pledge their undying love for each other.

Thank goodness the chirp of Matteo's phone broke the atmosphere.

'Ah…' His face broke into a grin as he opened his text message. '*Bel bambino*… Look.' He held the screen for Georgia to see. 'That's Arlo, waving hello to his uncle while he's having his bath.'

A fat, adorable baby with soap bubbles adorning his curly, dark hair was beaming at the camera, his chubby arms held up as if he was asking for a cuddle.

'Arlo?'

'My youngest nephew. Siena's first baby. Adrianna's pregnant again now. She'll be having her third, after a bit of a gap after the twins. I'll bet that will make Allegra jealous so I expect there'll be a new addition to her family soon as well.'

'How many nephews and nieces have you got?'

Matteo squinted as he concentrated and Georgia lost count as Italian names tumbled from his lips. He was scrolling through the photos on his phone at the same time. He leaned back on the couch for a moment in silence and Georgia watched the expression on his face change. His grin faded into something far more poignant and then he actually sniffed and rubbed at his fore-head as if fighting back tears.

'What?' Georgia asked quietly.

'It's a video. My nieces—Mita and Lia. It was their third birthday last year.'

He tapped the arrow on the centre of the screen as he tilted it towards her. The sound of giggles filled the room. Two identical small girls wearing frilly white dresses, with flowers in their hair, were climbing all over a man who was lying on the grass.

Matteo. He was laughing, too, as he scooped a child under each arm and sat up, kissing first one girl and then the other. One of the twins wriggled free and reached into the grass to pluck a daisy, which she triumphantly presented to her uncle.

'Grazie mille, tesoro. Ti amo...'

The words didn't need any translation. That expression on Matteo's face was tearing at a part of Georgia's heart.

'You really love kids, don't you?' she murmured, as the video ended.

'Of course. They are the most important thing

in the world. I ask for nothing more than to have the gift of my own family one day.' Matteo's smile was still poignant. 'No. I want more than that. I want to live to be a grandfather so that I don't leave my family with the sadness that we have.'

'You lost your father?'

'Many years ago. But I miss him every day.'

'And your mother?'

'My mama—Teresa Martini—is the proudest grandmother on the face of the earth. She welcomes every new baby as if it's the greatest gift possible. And she moves in with each of my sisters, every time. For at least a month after the birth.' Matteo's gaze was sombre. 'I'm sad that you don't have your mother to help you. It's a time when family comes together. Not just to celebrate but to make life easier.' He was frowning now. 'How will you manage, Georgie?'

She swallowed hard. 'I'll manage.'

'You must miss your mother so much.'

Georgia nodded slowly. As the birth of her babies drew closer she was missing that rock in her life more and more every day. She had to press her lips tightly together to cope with a stab of loss that was the biggest yet but she could still feel them tremble.

Only for a heartbeat, but Matteo must have seen her reaction because he lifted his hand and touched her lips with the pad of his thumb, his fingers cupping her cheek and jaw.

It was the most exquisitely tender gesture. In no way sexual but the response of her body and her heart had a kick that was far more powerful.

This…this felt like real love.

The kind that could last a lifetime?

'It's not long now, is it?'

'Um…no…' Her brain was too tired to try and do the maths that would keep her story straight but if she was a month more pregnant than she really was—as she'd allowed him to believe—that would mean she was due…

Oh, help…next week?

Was Matteo going to push her for an actual date?

No. He wasn't even looking at her. He was staring at her belly. Looking down, Georgia realised why. She was so used to the rippling sensations of her babies moving within her that she'd almost forgotten how extraordinary it was to *see* that movement as well as feel it.

She had long ago given up trying to wear anything like uniform pants. She had some comfortable maternity jeans on today, with the silky, stretch fabric of the insert a thin layer under the uniform polo shirt. A shirt that was visibly moving at the moment.

A look of something like reverence claimed Matteo's features and his gaze, when it captured hers, was the most intense she'd ever seen it.

'May I?' he asked softly.

It was impossible not to grant permission with the spell that that look was putting her under, but Georgia had to close her eyes as she felt the gentle weight of his hand outstretched on her belly.

Her skin was aware of the pressure on both sides. Her babies beneath and Matteo's hand on top.

Their father's hand.

It was too much. Too *wrong…*

He had to know the truth, didn't he?

She turned, tilting her head upwards to catch his gaze, her lips parting ready to release the words he had to hear.

But Matteo's head was closer than she'd realised. He had tears in his eyes as his gaze locked with hers.

And it took only the smallest movement for his lips to make contact with her own.

A brief, soft kiss. As tender as that touch of his fingers on her face had been.

She could feel his breath on her skin when they finally broke that kiss and his words were no more than a sigh.

'Ti amo, tesoro mio.'

Again, the words needed no translation. His eyes were telling her exactly what he'd whispered but maybe he hadn't intended her to understand them. Or even realise that they'd been audible.

How could she could tell him the truth now? If she said anything at all, it was more likely to be that she loved him as well.

And how could she say that when he didn't know the truth?

It was wrong, too.

Everything about this situation was so wrong. Perfect but twisted. And Georgia had no idea how to fix it.

Something of her dilemma must have shown on her face but Matteo didn't seem to be bothered. He was smiling at her.

'I excuse you the dishes,' he told her. 'Go to bed, *cara*. You're exhausted, yes?'

Georgia nodded. She swallowed hard.

'Thanks, Matteo.'

'For what? The food?' He waved a dismissive hand. 'It was nothing.'

'It wasn't nothing. It was…perfect.'

He was moving now. Collecting the empty plates as if this was just a part of a normal, everyday life.

'I'm glad you liked it. We'll do it again. We have plenty of time before I have to go back to Luke's apartment.'

Finally, Georgia could return the smile.

Plenty of time…

That was something else her mother used to say, too.

There's plenty of time, love.

Give it time…it'll be okay.

Time heals everything…

There was comfort to be found in those echoes of her mother's voice.

Hope, even.

Teresa Martini's lasagne had been a favourite for Matteo for as long as he could remember but it had just become even more significant in his life.

He'd taken a huge step towards his goal tonight.

He had been permitted to show Georgia a part of how he felt about her. The food he'd made for her hadn't been rejected. He'd been allowed to share the miracle of feeling the new life stirring within her.

He'd kissed her even. A kiss of nothing more than tenderness because anything else at this point in time was unthinkable.

And even though nothing had been said aloud,

he was quite certain that she had felt the same as he had—the profound depth of the connection between them. That she was thinking exactly what he was.

That she was in love…

It was enough of a declaration for now. He wasn't going to scare her again by trying to force something on her that she wasn't ready for.

Like too much of his company.

Or too much touching.

Or something stupid like offering to marry her again.

It was hard. Possibly the hardest thing he'd ever done, but he could take this slowly.

He could wait.

Until Georgia showed him that she was ready for more.

CHAPTER TEN

'THEY'LL BE THERE by now.'

'I know. Are you okay?'

'Why wouldn't I be?' Georgia picked up the pot Matteo had just put onto the draining board and started to dry it.

Matteo was scrubbing the next pot. 'There were a lot of tears at the airport yesterday. From Kate, anyway.' An eyebrow quirked in her direction. 'You are much tougher, I think.'

Georgia shrugged, her gaze sliding away from his. 'I just don't cry.'

'What…never? I have five sisters and a mother who cry all the time. *I* cry sometimes. It's nothing to be ashamed of.'

Yes. She could remember the times she had seen tears glinting in his eyes. Happy tears that were evoked by tapping into the enormous love he had for his family.

He had an infinite capacity for love, this man, didn't he?

When he'd had his hand on her belly that night, she could imagine that he was already feeling that love for a child that he still had no idea he had a close connection with.

There it was again.

That pressure.

The feeling that the account in the bank of time she'd believed she had was rapidly draining.

'Just because I don't cry on the outside doesn't mean I don't feel things. And Kate was upset that she couldn't be here to be my birth partner. She said that she'd tried to delay the start of her new job but just couldn't make it work when we can't be sure of an exact date.'

'It can't be far away.' Matteo's head turned again. 'Look how far back you have to stand from the bench.'

'I know. I won't be able to reach the steering wheel of my car soon because my arms won't be long enough. Just as well I'm allowed to work from home until I start my maternity leave officially.'

'That decides it, then.'

'Decides what?' Georgia could feel her eyes widening. Oh, help…the pressure had just kicked up another notch. How had she become so used to the luxury of thinking she had plenty of time to pick the right moment to tell Matteo what he had to know? Relaxing enough to find an excuse every time anything like an opportunity presented itself because she couldn't figure out a way of softening the shock by giving him some kind of a warning.

Opportunities like now, when they were sharing such a domestic task like washing dishes. When they were becoming so at ease with each other's company. Matteo had said he would never force himself on her and he'd proved that his word was his bond in the last couple of weeks. He'd been nothing more than a perfect flatmate.

A friend.

But that tone in his voice suggested something was about to change.

'I can't move back to Luke's apartment.'

'Oh?' It wasn't that Georgia wanted him to move out but the decisiveness of this statement was a little disturbing. What if he simply decided he had no intention of moving out of her life, full stop?

That was a battle she might not want to win. It could well be only wishful thinking but the idea of having Matteo in her life for ever had a glow of being as close to perfect as anything could get.

'Not yet, anyway. Not when you'll need someone to drive your car. To get groceries, for example.'

'I can order online. They deliver these days, you know.'

Matteo scowled at her. 'You might need to go to the hospital.'

A flutter of something like panic was trying to make itself felt. It wouldn't be perfect to have Matteo here for ever. Arguing with every decision she tried to make.

Taking control…

'I have a phone.' Her voice tightened. 'I could call you.'

'You might need to go in a hurry.'

Muscles in Georgia's jaw tightened. 'I can call an ambulance. I know a few people who work there and they'd get here pretty fast.'

'You *want* me to move out?'

If she said yes, would he pack his bag and leave instantly?

She wasn't ready for that. If he left, it would be even easier to avoid finding the right moment to tell him.

'Um…' Georgia bit her lip. This was getting onto dangerous territory. Her mind was spinning.

There was a soft chant as background to the conflicting thoughts.

Tell him…tell him…tell him…

'Ah…maybe not quite yet. There won't be much room when the…when the…'

'Baby arrives. I get it.'

But he didn't get it. Georgia had slammed on the mental brakes when the word 'bab*ies*' had been about to emerge. She'd sworn Kate to secrecy about that, on the grounds that she wanted to surprise everyone she knew. It was gratifying to know that she hadn't even told Luke. Or maybe she had. Maybe guys didn't pass on that sort of information because it wasn't interesting enough.

The moment he knew she was carrying twins, the game would be over. He'd know that she was bigger than expected for dates and that her pregnancy wasn't nearly as advanced as she'd let him assume. It would force the truth to come out.

'When is it due?'

'You never know with first babies.'

The response was evasive. Despite trying to make that chant go away by giving in to it, something was overriding her determination and making it impossible.

'They're rarely on time,' she added, a little desperately, 'and usually late.'

She hurriedly poked the last pot lid into the cupboard and then reached for the drainer to stand it upright at the end of the bench. But

Matteo was reaching for it as well and his hand caught her wrist.

'I need to know,' he said quietly. 'My mother and sisters are putting pressure on for me to go home for a few days. My work schedule will allow it in a couple of weeks but that could be just the wrong time. I want to be here for you.' He was making circles on her wrist with his thumb. 'I could be your birth partner instead of Kate if you like.'

The sensation of those circles on her skin was travelling up Georgia's arm like wildfire, obliterating every other thought that was still spinning. Up her arm, through her chest and straight down to an area low in her belly. It felt odd to experience a bolt of pure desire like this. Did pregnant woman still have sex when they were the size of a small elephant?

Would anyone other than the father of the baby even want to?

And, if he did, how exactly did they make it work?

She closed her eyes on a long blink as that

thought pushed the others away. She might know a way…

Matteo's thumb stilled. 'What is this from?' he asked quietly. 'This scar? I've been wondering about it…'

Someone throwing a bucket of iced water into her face could have had a similar effect on dousing that desire. For a moment, Georgia froze.

She'd already sensed that this was an opportunity to tell Matteo the truth. Or to at least tell him when her due date was so that he could work it out for himself and force a stop to this horrible procrastination. More than that, she realised that a better opportunity would never present itself. She was actually being given a chance to offer the foundation of any excuses for her deception before she dropped the bombshell of Matteo's impending fatherhood.

But, yet again, she couldn't do it.

Memory was such a bizarre thing. A smell could evoke a feeling of being straight back in your childhood, for instance. A thumb touching a jagged scar could suddenly burn, as though she could feel the pain of her arm being jammed in that car door all over again. She could definitely feel the shudder of remembered fear that had rippled down her spine.

She had to snatch her arm away.

'Don't…' she whispered. 'Please… I don't want to talk about it. I…*can't*…'

He couldn't let this go.

Okay, he'd said he wasn't going to force himself on her and he'd had no intention of pushing her at a pace she wasn't comfortable with.

But this was important.

No…it was more than that. Matteo's instincts were finely honed for signs and symptoms in patients that could mean that their condition was becoming critical.

This felt critical.

He followed Georgia into the sitting room. Already, she had picked up a sheaf of papers from work and seemed to be focused on reading them.

Shutting him out.

He sat beside her on the couch. Silently, for a

long moment, as he tried to think of what to say that wasn't going to make that barrier even more solid.

'If you want to watch television, that's fine.' Georgia's voice was tight. 'I can go and work in my room.'

'I don't want to watch television,' Matteo said quietly. 'I want to talk to you.'

She was silent.

'You don't have to tell me,' he added. 'But I'd really like you to. I care about you, *cara*—you know that. I get the feeling that that scar on your arm is more than just physical and... I want to know you better. To understand...'

It was that last word that seemed to find a chink in her armour. The papers drifted onto her lap as she closed her eyes.

'My arm got broken when I was five years old. A compound fracture. I've always told people that it happened when I fell off a pony but... it didn't. It came from having it slammed in a car door.'

'Dio mio...' Matteo's stomach churned at the thought of that pain. 'How did that happen?'

'My father did it.'

Now he felt sick. He'd been right, hadn't he, when he'd wondered if someone had abused Georgia to make her fearful of men in some way.

And that meant that the violence had been deliberate, not accidental.

'Right before he pushed my mother out of the way. So hard that she fell and hit her head on the pavement. She was still trying to get up as we drove away. I saw her out of the back window...'

Georgia Bennett never cried on the outside, but Matteo could hear the sobs of a terrified child behind her words.

He had to gather Georgia into his arms. To hold her. The papers slid from her lap onto the floor but she didn't seem to notice. She rested her head in the hollow beneath his shoulder and, slowly, started speaking again.

'He took me to a hospital, of course. The police came and I got taken home to my mother eventually but it was the start of fear for both of us. My father had become very religious and he made it his life's mission to make amends for the shame of the one-night stand that had brought me into the world, even though he'd wanted nothing to do with me when I was born. We had to keep moving. Trying to hide...'

It was an effort to keep the anger from his voice. 'Where is he now—this monster who was no father to you?'

'He's dead. He was killed in a fight. Stabbed by someone who disagreed with his lay preaching on a street corner.' He could feel the movement of Georgia's chest as she let her breath out in a sigh. 'My mum said it was karma.'

'It was certainly a good thing. You were safe...'

'I was still afraid. My mother developed epilepsy. The doctors thought it could have had something to do with a head injury that was never investigated properly that day I broke my arm. It was a petit mal seizure that probably caused her to step out onto a road...in front of a bus. I had just started work on the road after graduating from university.'

'Oh, no…you didn't find out by arriving on scene, did you?' Matteo's heart was breaking. He couldn't bear the thought of this story getting even worse.

'No…' Georgia tilted her head to look up at him. A hint of a smile tugged at one corner of her mouth. 'You're right… I hadn't actually ever thought of that. It *could* have been worse…'

No, it couldn't. Matteo tightened his hold on Georgia as he pressed a kiss to the top of her head. He'd guessed that there was something important about that scar. That it represented much more than simply a physical injury.

But this…

This was so huge he couldn't even begin to imagine how deeply it could have shaped a young life.

He needed to process this.

Thank goodness his instincts told him to back off. To take things slowly. To let Georgia choose when—or if—to invite him further into her life.

Telling him this had opened a door onto a space that was totally new.

A space that instinct told him nobody else had ever been allowed access to.

'There's something else I should tell you.'

He could feel the tension in her body now. Could feel her struggle.

'You don't have to,' he whispered. 'Not right now.' He stroked her hair. 'We have all the time in the world, *cara*. I'm not going anywhere. Not yet. I love you.'

She still felt incredibly tense. Trembling, almost, as if she was still afraid.

So he kept holding her, until he could feel that tension ebbing.

And then, when she looked up to catch her gaze, he kissed her again.

'You need to go to bed, *tesoro*. You need to sleep.'

'I don't want you to stop holding me right now,' she whispered. 'I love you, too.'

'I don't have to stop holding you.' Matteo murmured, but his words were coming out without him giving them much thought at all.

Georgia had spoken so quietly he wondered

whether he'd actually heard that last bit. Had she really just told him that she loved him? He wanted to ask if it was really true. If those barriers were truly vanquished. But that would make this moment more about him than Georgia, wouldn't it? If it was true, she would tell him again and he could be patient. Like his patience in getting closer to this woman he loved, it would be worth the wait.

'I could still hold you while you sleep, if you'd like that.'

And that would be all he would do. Just be there for her. Holding her. Willing her to believe that not all men were untrustworthy.

She was very, very still in his arms now.

And then she pushed herself up from the couch and stood there in front of him.

Her outstretched hand an invitation.

CHAPTER ELEVEN

GEORGIA BENNETT HAD believed that the love-making she had shared with Matteo Martini on that moonlit night in the Czech Republic had been the best she'd ever experienced.

She had been wrong.

The, oh, so gentle, heartbreakingly tender physical connection they'd inevitably shared when she'd led him to her bed that night had been something so extraordinary she was still stunned a week later.

Maybe it was due to the cathartic effect of talking about her childhood trauma for the first time. Of reliving such painful memories and then to find herself being cradled in arms that made her feel so safe.

She had definitely been about to tell Matteo the truth about her pregnancy right then because she had felt too drained to think about the consequences. She had still had to summon her courage, however, and he must have sensed how difficult it had been because he'd tried to make her feel even safer. He'd told her that she didn't need to say anything else and she'd let herself believe him. Let herself fall into that safety net of his arms a little further.

Just for that one night, she'd promised herself. She'd tell him tomorrow.

But tomorrow was always another day. Until today.

Georgia had known it was different from the moment she'd woken up at the sound of the front door of the cottage closing.

Something suddenly seemed urgent.

She was out of bed as fast as it was possible to be these days. Down the stairs faster than she should have, although she kept a firm hand on the bannister to keep her balance. She actually threw the door open, thinking she might have a chance to catch Matteo before he drove away, but she was too late.

'I'm too late,' she whispered aloud. 'What am I going to do?'

She paced the floor of the sitting room. It wasn't too late. She could tell him tonight. She would make dinner and tell Matteo how much she loved him.

And then she would tell him the truth about her pregnancy.

He was leaving to spend a few days with his family very soon and that might be a good thing because it could give him time to get used to the news.

With the decision definitively made, Georgia felt calmer. Not calm enough to crunch data and start writing up the first conclusions to do with her research project, however. She felt restless. Every time she sat down to try and work, she would think of something else that needed doing. Like putting the rubbish out and wiping down the kitchen bench and then—oddly—taking every single thing out of the fridge so she could simply clean the shelves and put it all back again.

She was nervous, she decided, when she was

dusting the top of the bookshelf in the sitting room—a task that hadn't been done for so long it would have been easy to write her name in the film covering the wood. No. She was impatient. She was finally ready to do the thing she should have done a long time ago and the hours were passing too slowly.

She spent most of the afternoon out in the garage, which was used for storage rather than as shelter for cars. It had a few old pieces of furniture in there. And the chest freezer that there was no room for in the house. Over the last month or more, it had also been used as a place to hide the fact that she was collecting so much baby gear. Two bassinets. Two car seats. A small mountain of baby clothes and nappies.

It needed sorting. To see what else she was missing.

By evening, that big task was completed and the house had never been so clean and tidy. Maybe the smell in the kitchen wasn't on a par with Matteo's lasagne but it would be good enough by the time the steaks were sizzling and could add their aroma to the baked potatoes already in the oven.

Georgia's feet hurt after all the pacing about she had been doing all day.

Her back hurt, too, which was hardly surprising.

Not that it mattered. She forgot about any pain the moment she heard the tyres of Matteo's car crunching to a halt on the gravel driveway.

Until the moment that the handle of the door turned and he was stepping into the kitchen.

She couldn't think of anything *but* the pain then.

Because it had suddenly blossomed into a cramp that made her gasp aloud with its intensity. Made it imperative that she get hold of the back of that chair beside the little table so that she had some support and didn't crumple to the floor.

'Georgie?' She could hear the thump of Matteo's satchel hitting the floor. 'Oh...*no*...'

He must be able to see what she was feeling— the rush of fluid down her legs that warned her that her waters had just broken.

The pain was still blinding her and Matteo was making it worse by making her move. Half-carrying her into the sitting room and then easing her onto the floor.

'Don't move,' he told her.

Georgia covered her eyes with her hand. She couldn't move even if she wanted to. How could this be happening so fast, with so little warning?

The first contraction had barely begun to fade when another one started.

She heard Matteo's voice. Sharp, clipped instructions to the control room at the rescue base as he demanded an ambulance.

She *had* had warning, she realised, groaning aloud.

That restlessness hadn't been impatience to get her confession to Matteo over with. And that back pain hadn't been simply due to too much time on her feet.

Her doctor had even warned her last week, when she'd gone in for her antenatal check, that this could happen.

'It's twins,' he'd reminded her. *'They're very*

likely to come a bit early. Things are getting pretty crowded in there.'

Matteo was crouching beside her now, a stack of the towels Georgia had refolded earlier today in his arms.

'The ambulance is on its way,' he told her. 'We'll probably hear the siren in no time at all.'

'I don't think it's going to get here on time.' Georgia was frightened now. 'I can feel something happening. Oh, my God... I have to *push...*'

'It's okay...we've got this...' She could feel Matteo's hands as she pulled her legs up. Ripping her clothing clear. Pushing *back...?*

Of course...he was trying to slow a precipitous birth to keep the baby safe.

Georgia tried to pant and slow things down herself but her body wasn't listening. Another contraction and another overwhelming urge to push so hard that she had red spots dancing on the back of her eyelids and a roaring sound in her ears.

It didn't drown out the sound of Matteo's calm voice, though.

'Almost there… You're doing great… That's *it*…'

And then another sound cut through the noise in her head.

The warbling cry of a newly born infant.

Georgia struggled to push herself up on her elbows.

'It's a little girl,' Matteo told her. 'And she's gorgeous. Look…'

He was holding her baby in his bare hands. A tiny, wrinkled red face was screwed up, ready to emit another cry.

'You've done it, Georgie…she's okay. Everything's okay…'

'No…' Georgia's head dropped back to the floor. 'It's not over… *Oh*…' It was her turn to cry aloud as a new contraction built. 'It's twins, Matteo…'

'*What?* How could you not have told me that?'

What she hadn't told Matteo was the least of her worries at this moment. This pain was unbelievably intense. Matteo's voice blurred into the sound of her firstborn crying. Her own cries. The faint background wail of an approaching siren...

Matteo had never been this afraid in his career.

He'd attended many births but this was so different, he felt like he had no idea of what he was doing.

He could see his hands doing all the things they needed to be doing but it was like watching hands that belonged to someone else.

His brain was detached.

Reeling...

Twins? How could Georgia have kept such important information a secret?

They'd become so close since she'd shared the terrible story behind that scar on her arm.

She'd wanted to tell him something else that night, hadn't she?

But he'd stopped her.

Why?

Because he'd known that whatever it was she had been about to say was difficult? That maybe she hadn't really wanted to tell him at all?

Again…*why*…?

Any baby was a miracle. Twins were something very special. He knew that. His sister had been doubly blessed with little Mita and Lia. It was something to celebrate, not hide…

Unless she had believed that, for some reason, it put her in jeopardy?

Somehow he kept his hands moving. The baby girl was small but looked fine. She was breathing well and nicely pink. He wrapped her in soft, clean towels to keep her warm and then turned his attention back to the arrival of her brother or sister. A breech delivery, this one, which kicked his focus sharply back into place. This one had to happen slowly. Gently.

He heard the sounds of the ambulance crew arriving, the bang of the door and the rattle of stretcher wheels behind him.

'Don't push,' he warned Georgia. 'It's very important.' He turned his head and spoke to the first paramedic to enter the room. 'Grab some cushions off the couch, please. I need to get her hips higher than her shoulders.'

'It's a breech?'

'Yep.'

'You're doing a great job, Georgie,' the second paramedic said, depositing an oxygen cylinder and pack of gear onto the floor. 'Couldn't wait for us, huh? Looks like we're only going to be a taxi to get you into hospital.'

Georgia wasn't listening. 'I have to push,' she groaned.

'Okay…we've got this…' Matteo cradled the tiny buttocks that were on the move. A boy this time…and…thank goodness, he was going to be all right. His tiny limbs were twitching as soon as his head was delivered, his chest heaving as he made the immense effort of sucking in his very first breath.

'I can't believe it's *twins*.' The paramedic who seemed to know Georgia very well had picked up the baby wrapped in towels. 'Good grief, champ, you're good at keeping secrets, aren't you?'

Matteo was lifting her son in his arms, ready to place him skin to skin with his mother as the other paramedic clamped and cut the cord. His gaze snagged Georgia's.

Yes…she was good at keeping secrets all right…

'Are they full term?' the paramedic asked.

It felt as though Georgia was struggling to pull her gaze away from his but couldn't quite manage it.

'No,' she said quietly. 'They're nearly five weeks early.'

And there it was.

The ground seemed to be slipping away from beneath Matteo's feet as he found the answer to all those unanswered questions.

This was why Georgia hadn't told him.

Maybe it was also why he had shied away from allowing her to.

Because, even in the midst of the miracle of new life, it felt as if something important had just died.

The maternity ward of this old Edinburgh hospital was never really quiet.

Even in the earliest hours of this new day, there were sounds to be heard. The squeak of wheels or soft-soled shoes in the corridor, a phone ringing somewhere or a cry from a hungry baby.

That sound generated an odd tingling sensation in Georgia's breasts and took her straight back to the miracle of feeding her babies for the first time, less than an hour ago, up in the neonatal intensive care unit.

She wanted to be there now. Had asked that she be allowed to stay beside their incubators all night, but the staff had been kind but firm. She needed to rest. She could come back as soon as she'd had a few hours of sleep and, in the meantime, her babies would have the very best of care.

She didn't need to worry. Her babies were both healthy—just small enough to need their breathing monitored for a day or two. So she'd left them—those two tiny bundles, one with a soft, woolly blue hat and one with a pink one.

Not that there was any chance of sleeping just yet, despite an exhaustion like nothing she had ever experienced before. Propped up against her pillows, Georgia was floating on the sea of this huge new life, trying to catch and process everything that had happened in the last, tumultuous hours.

The fear that had come with that unexpectedly early and precipitous birth.

The fact that Matteo had delivered his own children.

The bombshell of him having to find that out in what was probably the worst possible way.

But all those things paled in comparison to the knowledge that she was now a mother. That her precious babies were healthy.

Her *babies*…

This room felt incredibly empty. The need to get up and go back to where they were was so strong that Georgia actually pushed the covers back on her bed and began to move, as she turned her head to look towards the light coming through the open door of her room.

Two things made her freeze.

One was the painful cramping in her belly.

The other was the silhouette of a silent figure standing in her doorway.

For a long, long moment, they simply stared at each other. As her eyes adjusted to the contrast in light, Matteo's features became clearer and Georgia's heart sank like a stone as she saw how tight they were.

As frozen as her body felt right now.

He stepped closer. Just as far as the end of the bed. Into the gentle light from her bedside table.

And now she could see his eyes and that made it all so much worse because he looked absolutely...devastated.

His words, when he finally spoke, were quiet. Calm even. He was just announcing a fact.

'You lied to me.'

'Not directly...'

A soft snort from Matteo made her ashamed of even going there.

'You told me you were already pregnant the night that we were first together.'

Georgia swallowed hard. 'Technically, I was. At the end...'

'Stop this.' The flicker of real anger in his eyes sent a chill down Georgia's spine. 'I don't want to hear any more of your half-truths. You lied to me, even if it was just letting me believe something that wasn't right, and you know it. Unless…' He was closing his eyes as he spoke. 'Unless there was someone else at Rakovi? And you didn't know for sure who the father was? Is that what this cover-up was all about?'

'No.' That he could even think that was astonishingly painful. 'There was no one else, Matteo. It was only you. It could only have been you.'

And she wasn't only referring to the fathering of her babies. Matteo was the only man she could ever feel like this about. *Love* this much…

His eyes snapped open. 'So these babies *are* mine, then.'

It had been painful enough when he'd been speaking with his eyes closed. This was way harder, being unable to look away from him and having to absorb his pain on top of her own.

'Yes, Matteo. They're yours.'

'You've been lying to me every minute of every day that I've been with you, then, haven't you?'

How could she even begin to try and explain why? Or to tell him that she'd just been waiting for the combination of the right moment and enough courage? That she loved him…

He wouldn't want to hear any of it. Not now.

It was too late.

'I'm…sorry,' she whispered.

Another huff of sound came from Matteo. The note of something like despair in it took her down to a new low.

'You've stolen something from me that I can never, ever get back.' There was a moment's silence where she could see that Matteo was fighting for control. 'The knowledge that my first baby was being born. My first *children*…' His control slipped and his voice cracked. 'I held those babies as they took their first breaths and…and I didn't know that…that they were *mine*…'

There was nothing that she could say. He was right. She *had* stolen something so huge it was unforgiveable. It made no difference at all now that she hadn't intended to. That even a few hours more would have changed everything.

The silence was unnerving.

'Have…have you been to see them?'

'Not yet. I had to come here first. To find out the truth.'

Not to find out how she was?

Did that mean he didn't care any more?

Had this revelation changed everything between them to that extent?

The emotion of everything that had happened today and what was happening now were becoming too much. A heavy weight that was pressing down on Georgia and making it hard to breathe. The fear that she was losing Matteo was the final straw and she had no resources left to fight the painful prickling behind her eyes.

She never cried.

But right now a huge, fat tear was slowly trickling down the side of her nose. *She* should be caring for those babies.

With Matteo by her side.

It was never going to happen, though, was it?

'I can't trust you.' The words were weighted with sadness. Disappointment. Heartache. 'You're the mother of my children and the woman I love but…but I can't trust you. You told me that you loved me… But maybe you lied about that, too.'

Georgia rolled her head from side to side, denying his assumption, but Matteo wasn't looking at her now. He was turning away.

And then she rewound the words she had just heard a little further. He could still say he loved her? A tiny flare of something like hope flickered in the darkness of her fear.

'Please don't go… Stay…'

Matteo shook his head. A single, sharp movement. 'I can't. I need time to think.' He stepped towards the door. 'And…I need to go and meet my children.'

Georgia nodded slowly. 'Of course.' She rubbed at the unfamiliar moisture on her face and started to slide off the bed. 'I'll come with you.'

She needed to be there when Matteo was with their babies. To share his first moment with them knowing he was their father.

Because it was huge. As big as their first moments in the world.

'No.' The single word was like a physical blow. 'I don't want you to come with me. I… I can't think straight when I'm near you. I need to do this on my own.'

She pulled in a shaky breath. 'Will you come back…later?'

The question seemed to surprise Matteo. He paused but didn't turn around as he reached the door.

'I don't know.'

The room had felt empty before, because her babies weren't with her.

It felt infinitely more empty after their father had left.

Another tear rolled down Georgia's face. And then another.

Maybe he would never come back…

She sank back onto her pillows, wrapping her arms around one of them because she really, really needed something to hold.

Exhaustion was bleeding into the darkness of

this empty room and softening the edges of the awful aching in her heart.

She could escape all of it, couldn't she? At least for a little while. She just needed to give in to this crippling tiredness. And maybe…when she woke up…she might even find it had all just been a nightmare.

They knew who Matteo was as soon as he arrived at the neonatal intensive care unit and introduced himself.

Somehow, that astonished him.

Georgia had been lying to him for so long and yet she'd announced the truth to the world by officially naming him as the father of these children? That she had was confirmed by the labels on the incubators he was led towards.

Bennett/Martini: Twin One and Twin Two.

Not that this public confession made any difference.

Not when she'd had a million opportunities to tell *him* and she had chosen not to. Matteo was still reeling. Trapped in the darkness of what felt like an ultimate betrayal.

'You can hold them,' the nurse told him. 'They're only in the incubators to make use of the apnoea alarms. Sit here and I'll take them out for you.'

Matteo sat in the comfortable armchair and the nurse lifted one tiny bundle and then the other, to place the twins in his arms.

'I'll leave you alone to get to know each other for a bit.' She smiled. 'But do you want me to take a photo first?'

'Not yet…'

He knew he wouldn't be able to smile. He might even have tears rolling down his face if the wash of emotion he was feeling right now was anything to go by.

This was…

Like nothing he could identify.

He could relate to it, of course. Like when he'd held Arlo shortly after his birth and had experienced that wave of love and pride for the new member of the Martini clan.

But this was so different.

These were *his* very own children.

He had just stepped into his long-held dream of being a father.

No. He hadn't stepped. He'd been pushed in such a dramatic fashion it felt like he'd been hit by a truck he hadn't seen coming.

But that didn't seem to be making any difference right now. He was here and…and it was… amazing…

He could feel the weight of each baby nestled in the crook of each arm. He could see their little button noses and wisps of dark hair from beneath the blue and pink hats. He could hear the adorable snuffling sounds and soft squeaks of tiny humans who were getting used to their new existence of living and breathing on their own.

They were only a couple of hours old.

And it didn't seem to matter so much now that he hadn't known he was their father as they'd entered the world. A lot of fathers missed the actual delivery of their children, especially when they arrived unexpectedly early. He could have known and then missed the moment by something as simple as being caught in a traffic jam. Georgia hadn't stolen something irrevocable from him because it wasn't making any difference to this bonding process. To this genesis of being someone totally new.

A *father*...

The love he felt for these tiny beings was swamping him.

It was the most beautiful thing in the world but...but there was a fear there as well.

The fear of something bad happening to them.

Matteo had always been protective of the people he loved but this new determination to guarantee safety was so fierce it was painful.

Did Georgia feel like this, too?

Of course she did.

She had probably felt like this from the moment she'd known she was carrying these babies.

He'd seen the fear in her eyes that night, hadn't he? When he'd surprised her by arriving to be Luke's best man at his wedding.

She hadn't wanted him to know the truth because…

Because she'd lived her whole life being afraid of her own father.

Would he break his own iron-clad rules of not being dishonest if he thought it could be the guarantee that would keep these precious babies safe?

Yes. In a heartbeat.

And Georgia had been right, hadn't she? Technically, she hadn't *told* a lie. She had done what he might have done himself, if he'd believed he was protecting these babies.

She had been prepared to walk away from the love they had found for each other, if that had been what it took to keep her babies safe.

Did that mean he could forgive her?

Did he love her that much? As much as the love he was feeling for his first-born children?

An image of Georgia filled his mind. Sitting on that bed looking so pale and exhausted.

Looking as afraid as she'd been when he'd first arrived back in her life.

Crying…

She never cried. He should have taken her into his arms as soon as he'd seen that tear trickling down her face but, instead, he'd only been thinking of himself.

Of how hurt he was by the deception. How angry he was that he'd had the most important moment in his life stolen from him.

Matteo bent his head, to place the softest kiss ever on the forehead of his son. And another one for his daughter.

Nothing had been stolen from him. He had, in fact, received the biggest gift he could ever get.

He turned his head to catch the glance of the nurse.

He was ready to have that photograph taken now.

Then he was going to take the image back down to the maternity ward and show it to Georgia.

And he was going to tell her that he understood. That he had already forgiven her.

He just had to hope that she loved him enough to forgive him for his selfishness now. That there was a way they could get past it all and make this brand-new family what it could be.

Perfect...

They knew who he was on the maternity ward, too, but the nurse who intercepted him wasn't about to make things easy.

'Georgia's finally asleep,' she told him. 'Please don't disturb her. It's really important that she gets some rest.'

'I won't disturb her,' he promised. 'Let me just sit in her room with her so I can be there when she wakes up.'

But the nurse shook her head. 'Go home. Get some rest yourself and come back in the morning. It's not that long to wait.'

It felt too long.

Matteo stood in the corridor of the ward, reluctant to leave by pushing his way through the swing doors. Not that he intended to go home. He would wait in the seating area near the elevators.

He still had his phone in his hand and it was a comfort to look at that image that had just been recorded of him holding those bundles that were his babies. His smile said all that needed to be said about how he felt. About how much love he had to give.

He could send the image to Georgia, couldn't he? Even if he wasn't here the moment she woke up, she could see that image and she would know that he was coming back.

Maybe she would even believe that he had already forgiven her.

But the text wouldn't send.

Oh…of course. He'd put his phone on airplane mode so that it couldn't interfere with any hospital equipment like IV pumps.

He flicked it back, but before he could try sending the image again he heard the sound of an incoming text. And a buzz that indicated a missed call.

Two missed calls…no, make that four…*five*?

What on earth was going on?

He went to voicemail and waited. Had his family somehow known what he hadn't known? That he'd become a father?

No. His sister's voice was anything but happy.

'Matti? Where are you? Why aren't you answering your phone?'

The stifled sob he could hear sent a chill down Matteo's spine.

'You need to come home. Mama's in hospital... we think that she's had a heart attack...'

It was easy to push those swing doors open now.

Not just to leave the maternity ward but to do so at a run.

CHAPTER TWELVE

'YOU'RE GOING HOME? *Already?*' Kate sounded shocked on the other end of the line.

'The twins are doing really well. Everybody's happy that they're ready to go home. Sean's coming later this afternoon to collect us all.'

'But the house won't be ready.'

'It is. I ducked home for a while yesterday and took all the stuff out of the garage. And I've got the car seats and lots of clothes here. We're all set.'

'Where's Matteo?' Luke was on speakerphone with Kate. 'He'll be able to help.'

'In Italy.' Georgia had to squeeze her eyes tightly shut. Her hormones were all over the place now and it seemed that she was going to make up for all those years of never crying. 'His mother's in hospital, apparently. He sent a text message from the airport. A very brief one. I don't know what's wrong with his mother or anything.'

Luke was laughing. 'Yeah…he's always treated text messaging like a pager from work. Succinct information with no frills and nothing personal.'

'Yep.' The message was burned into Georgia's brain by now.

Heading to Italy. Mother in hospital. Back when I can. Need to talk.

'He's good with Skype, though. You could try that.'

No, she couldn't. She couldn't force a conversation on Matteo when he needed time to think.

When he couldn't think straight when he was near her.

That was one of the two things she was hanging onto at the moment—that he still had to have some fairly powerful feelings for her if it messed with his head that much. And that meant that there was still hope…

'Send more photos of those adorable babies,'

Kate put in. 'And have you come up with some names yet?'

'Yes, I will,' Georgia promised. 'And, no, I can't think of names. My brain is mush.'

She had come up with a hundred names but couldn't make a decision. Because it wasn't just hers to make? And she couldn't send them the photo that had come with Matteo's text, of him with his babies. Not until they knew the truth and when they found that out wasn't up to her. It had to be Matteo's choice. Maybe if it had just been Kate she was talking to, she would have confessed everything but it seemed like Kate wasn't just Kate any more. She was part of Luke and Kate—an inseparable team. And Luke's first loyalties after Kate had to lie with his best friend.

The sooner Matteo told them the better, as far as Georgia was concerned.

She was over keeping secrets.

She didn't want to be the person that Matteo had been describing the other night. Dishonest. Untrustworthy…

Oh, man…another bout of tears was imminent.

'I'd better let you go,' she said quickly. 'It must be the middle of the night for you guys.'

'It is but it doesn't matter. Call anytime…and *good* luck.'

'I'll be fine.'

'Of course you will. Oh, but I do wish I was there to help…'

Less than two days later and Georgia was also wishing that Kate was there to help.

The home help for several hours a day that was part of her ongoing maternity care had left and she was, once again, alone in her house with the babies. There were still a dozen things she needed to do, like fold the overflowing basket of washing in the corner of the sitting room, put away the rest of the online grocery order that had been delivered moments after her home help had gone and check her neglected email and phone messages.

Georgia stood in the middle of the sitting room, pushing the twin pushchair both babies were lying in back and forth as she sang a lullaby. The singing was on autopilot because her brain was busy trying to prioritise her list. As soon as she could be sure they were really asleep she could do the first thing on that list, but after last night she knew she might have a lot less time than she needed so she had to make sure she tackled the most important task first. Maybe it was finding some food. She was *starving*…

And then one of the babies started crying.

Her daughter, who still didn't have a name.

Picking her up, she held her cradled against her shoulder and tried to keep rocking the pushchair with her other hand.

Lucy? Katy?… Bella?

She liked Bella a lot.

But Bella Bennett? No, it didn't sound right.

Bella Martini sounded so much better.

And, just like that, her thoughts shot back to Matteo, along with a stabbing sensation in her chest that felt a lot like loss.

The baby was still crying, rubbing her face on her mother's shoulder, that tiny open mouth communicating as clearly as any words.

Georgia sat on the couch and offered her breast to the hungry baby, still trying to keep the pushchair rocking, first with her foot on the axle and then with a free hand once her daughter was latched on.

For a few moments at least, a blessed silence fell.

'He's coming back,' she whispered, her forefinger gently stroking the cheek of the baby she held. 'Your daddy. He would never abandon you. He loves you.'

She might be saying it simply to reassure herself but Georgia believed her words. Because of that photo. Because Matteo had looked so happy holding the babies. He looked like the proudest father ever. He might not trust her and he might even want to fight for custody of his children but, right now, that didn't scare Georgia the way she would have expected it to.

Because she had seen something else in that photo. That Matteo was experiencing that same kind of life-changing, all-encompassing love that she had been swamped with from the moment she had first held both of her babies.

Because she wanted him to be part of his children's lives.

She wanted him to be part of *her* life, in whatever way they could make it work.

How weird was that?

The complete opposite of what Kate had referred to as her 'hare-brained' scheme. The one where she gave up on men completely and was going to have a baby all by herself…

What would her mother have said about that?

Probably something like, *'Be careful what you wish for, love…'*

Tears gathered so easily these days. Maybe it was just hormones. Or maybe a dam had been breached that night she had told Matteo about the scar on her arm and she was going to have to release all the tears that had accumulated in the years of being banished.

If only she'd been brave enough to tell him the whole truth that night.

She was feeling a little bit sorry for herself at the moment, in all honesty.

She *had* given up on that scheme to find an unwitting sperm donor at the competition.

But look at her now…

Alone. With *two* babies. She'd been so happy to find out that she was pregnant. So confident that she would be able to cope. Still so determined that she didn't want their father having any influence on how she brought them up. Of being any kind of a threat.

But this was Matteo she was talking about.

And that was why everything had changed.

She loved him so much. And love like that had its roots very firmly buried in trust. Her heart knew that. It was just that her head had decided to override it for far too long.

Rocking wasn't cutting it for her baby boy and within seconds whimpers from the pushchair became a heartbreaking wail.

She used her little finger to gently break the suction on her breast, feeling guilty as she did so. Her daughter's eyes were drifting shut and maybe she would sleep for long enough for her brother to be fed. But Georgia could feel how damp her nappy was as she laid the baby into the nest of cushions on the couch beside her and her eyes were open again. She might have fallen asleep on the breast but her damp bottom was obviously bothering her now. Or maybe she hadn't had enough milk yet?

She'd seen pictures of women breastfeeding twins at the same time but how on earth did they manage it? Surely the only way it could be possible would be to have someone else to help position them?

Both babies were crying now.

And so was Georgia.

She desperately needed help and she missed her mum so much it hurt.

She missed Kate, too.

But most of all she missed Matteo.

The noise level in this small house was so overpowering it was astonishing that Georgia could hear anything else—like the slamming of a car door. Maybe she noticed because it happened more than once.

Was it Sean, perhaps? Or some of her other friends from work?

Whoever it was, she wasn't going to be able to pretend that she was coping brilliantly but she could, at least, try. She pushed tangled tresses of her hair back from her face and then scrubbed at those tell-tale tear tracks.

She could hear voices outside now.

A firm, male voice, speaking in... *Italian*?

Georgia's heart leapt. Matteo was here.

He had come back...

But he wasn't alone. She caught a snatch of female voices, who seemed to be arguing with him.

Her heart dropped like a stone from the astonishing height it had just achieved.

This had been her worst fear, hadn't it? Having to face an entire family of angry Italians who were determined to claim their own.

Somehow, she managed to scoop both her babies into her arms and, as if they sensed the significance of what was happening, they both stopped crying as the door opened and their father walked in.

One look at the way Matteo was standing told her that he was as tense as he had been the last time she had seen him, when he'd come into her hospital room. And one look at his face told her that he had, indeed, come to claim his own.

The question that she couldn't begin to find an answer to, however, was whether *she* could possibly be included in that number.

'I need you to tell me something,' Matteo said quietly.

He had said that to her once before, hadn't he? In the car that night after Kate and Luke's wedding. When he'd been about to ask her if she'd already known she was pregnant the night they'd first made love.

And she had felt as if any safety barriers around her had just evaporated. That she was standing on the edge of a cliff and the slightest wrong move would be catastrophic.

She was on that cliff edge again but this time the catastrophe would be if Matteo was going to vanish from her life, not insist on being a part of it.

'Were you telling the truth when you said you loved me?'

And here it was. An opportunity to tell Matteo the absolute truth and Georgia didn't hesitate for even a heartbeat.

'*Yes*. With all my heart, Matteo. From the moment I met you, I think. And for always...'

For a long, long moment he was silent, his gaze holding hers from across the room.

The corners of his mouth curved as if he was about to smile and, in that moment, Georgia knew that everything was going to be all right. Better than all right, judging by the way her heart was soaring again. She needed to learn to trust what she could feel and she wasn't going to let her head argue the toss about anything this time. Matteo still loved her. It looked as though he had even forgiven her.

But both babies chose that moment to start crying again and, at the same time, a sound from behind made him turn his head.

'I said to wait outside, Mama… That Georgie and I need to talk…'

'She can't wait,' another voice said, in heavily accented but perfect English. 'And neither can I.' A tall woman with a tumble of black, curly hair and a rounded belly of early pregnancy edged past Matteo and walked straight towards Georgia.

'I'm Adrianna,' she said, her smile lighting up her face. 'Matti's sister. It's so good to finally meet you, Georgia. He's told us so much about you.' Her gaze dropped to the bundles cradled protectively in Georgia's arms. 'Oh, Mama…you have to see. It's Mita and Lia all over again…'

'I have to find somewhere to put this lasagne. Matteo…where's the oven?'

'I'm sorry, Georgie,' he said. 'I tried to stop them. I said I had to talk to you first, and make sure you were okay with this…'

There were tears rolling down Adrianna's face now as she gazed at the twins. 'They're just *perfect*, aren't they?'

There weren't many people who could look at

screaming babies who needed both feeding and changing and describe them as perfect, but the upward glance from Matteo's sister told Georgia that this woman knew exactly how she felt about her babies. And how stressful this was.

'Let me help,' she said softly. 'Please?'

'And me.' Teresa Martini was an older, smaller version of Adrianna. With the same smile that was brimming over with love. 'My heart was broken when I heard that you didn't have your mama to help. Don't blame Matteo. We couldn't let him come back without us.'

'But… I thought you were sick. That you were in hospital…'

'Pff…' Teresa flapped a hand. 'It was nothing. I'm fine.'

'They thought it was a heart attack.' Matteo had come close. 'And then that it might be angina. They kept her in to do all the tests but she *is* fine. It was something muscular, probably.' But he was looking worried. 'This is too much, isn't it? I knew it would be. I tried to tell them.'

Both women were reaching for the babies.

It should have been terrifying and Georgia knew that, if she wanted it, Matteo would tell his mother and sister to back off.

But it wasn't terrifying.

It felt like…family…

And if her babies were being held for a little while by a loving aunt and grandmother, then there would be nothing in the way of Matteo holding *her*…

'So… Isabella Kate, then? Bella for short?'

'*Sì…*'

They'd had to wait until they were alone together, after a taxi had been summoned to take Matteo's mother and sister to their hotel, to start talking about private things. Like how much they loved each other and how sorry they were that things hadn't been handled well and, of course, what they were going to name their precious babies.

It had taken too long but how could he complain when he could see how the first representatives of his family were taking Georgia and the twins into their hearts so willingly. Nurturing them with food and love and laughter and tears.

And Georgia hadn't been totally overwhelmed by this small invasion, even when they'd taken over completely and tidied the house by putting away groceries and folding washing while they waited for the lasagne that his mother had carried all the way from Italy to get thoroughly heated in the oven.

The meal could have been in a courtyard garden back home, with grapevines overhead and tired children sleeping in corners like puppies. A little bit of Italy in rural Scotland. The best of both his worlds because Italy was his homeland and Scotland was the homeland of the woman who was the centre of his world now.

Matteo blinked hard to prevent his vision being blurred by any tears. He stooped to place the softest kiss imaginable onto the swaddled bundle in the bassinet. '*Ciao*, Bella,' he murmured. 'Sleep tight.'

His arm tightened around Georgia's waist as

he straightened. They both shifted their gaze to the neighbouring bassinet.

'And our son?'

'Bella was my choice. Maybe you should choose his name.'

'You've given Bella a name of your closest friend. Maybe he could be Luca? And Pietro after my father for his middle name.'

'Oh… I love it.' Georgia's sigh sounded like relief. She followed his example and bent to kiss their baby boy. '*Ciao*, Luca,' she whispered. 'You sleep tight, too. Please…?'

She was smiling as she turned back to Matteo.

'They're not going to believe it.'

'Who?'

'Kate and Luke. That we've named our babies after them.' Georgia's smile dimmed. 'They're not going to believe any of it. Kate's going to be so hurt that I never told her the truth.'

'She didn't know?' Matteo was astonished. According to his sisters, best female friends told each other absolutely anything.

'She knew I was having twins. She has no idea who the father is but I think she decided it was a New Zealand guy that we'd met the first night at the competition.'

'Yes…she told me something like that.' Matteo wrapped his arms around Georgia. 'Did she know about your father? The story about your scar?'

'No…' Georgia's response was quiet. 'You're the only person I've ever told about that.'

He just held her for a long moment after that. It made him feel honoured that she had trusted him enough to share something so huge. That he was the only person she had trusted this much.

'I don't really want to tell her now either.'

It made him feel even more protective, too.

'You don't have to. It's our secret now. Nobody has to know when, or how, I knew I'd become a father. Or that things were…difficult between us for a while. All they need to know is that everything is as it should be now. And the date for our wedding, of course.'

He felt Georgia go very still in his arms.

'You still want to marry me?'

He eased his hold so that he could capture her gaze.

'I knew that you were the woman I was destined to marry from the first moment I saw you.' His lips quirked. 'I didn't expect to have to fight so hard to win, mind you. I had to fight myself as well as you.'

Her face crinkled apologetically. 'I messed up, didn't I?'

'*Sì...*' But Matteo could feel his smile trying harder to emerge. 'But I understand why. When I held our...when I held Bella and Luca for the first time, I understood how powerful love can be. How it can make you do things that you might never really *want* to do. How someone else's safety can be so much more important than your own.'

He tilted his head so that his forehead rested against Georgia's.

'That's how much I love you, too, *tesoro*... I want to keep you safe and love you. For always and for ever.' He swallowed hard. 'So…will you marry me?'

'Yes. A thousand times, yes. Or should I say *sì*?' There was laughter in her eyes as she lifted her head. 'I'd already decided that Bella Martini sounded much better than Bella Bennett. I'm going to have to learn to speak Italian, aren't I?'

'You might even want to live in Italy. We have so many things to talk about but all I want to do right now is to lie down with you. And hold you. And never let you go.'

'You might have to let me go sooner than you think. You have no idea how much our babies love their food.'

'They're half-Italian. Of course they love their food. They'll be eating Mama's lasagne before we know it.'

'Mmm…' Georgia licked her lips. 'I might just go and eat a bit more of it myself.'

'I should call her. She will want to know the names of her newest grandchildren.'

'We should call Kate and Luke, too.'

They held each other's gaze. Matteo could see that Georgia was thinking the same thing he was.

That this was their time. A bubble that they would never have again. The first, amazing moments of believing that they could hold onto happiness like this for ever.

It was too special to share with anyone else.

They both spoke at the same time as they wrapped their arms around each other and sank into that closeness like no other.

'Tomorrow...'

* * * * *